Fooling Around With Cinderella

To Cheryl,
Sending you lots
of Cinderella magic
for 2016!
Love, Stacy

STACY JUBA

Cover, design and typesetting by Mark Juba

Also By Stacy Juba

Adult Mystery/Romantic Suspense

Twenty-Five Years Ago Today

Sink or Swim

Young Adult

Dark Before Dawn

Face-Off

Children's

The Flag Keeper

Teddy Bear Town Children's Bundle

More titles in the *Storybook Valley Series* coming soon. Sign up for Stacy's newsletter at www.stacyjuba.com for new book releases.

Chapter One

Jaine Andersen couldn't stop staring at the framed poster of Cinderella outside the castle. Cylindrical towers and turrets ascended into the sapphire sky, lofty mountains rising in the background. Her hand poised in an elegant wave, Cinderella beamed toward the camera. Ornate script flowed across the right side of the glossy photograph.

"Follow your heart, dream big, and you will find the magic."

"Okay, Jaine, time to find the magic," she mumbled, shifting in her seat.

"Interesting. What magic are you hoping to find?" a masculine voice asked behind her.

The kind that erases someone's memory and lets you start over? Nice going, Jaine.

Squirming, Jaine clutched the black leather portfolio case in her lap as Dylan Callahan closed his office door. He sat down at a battered desk strewn with papers, her eyes tracking his every movement. Forget Cinderella's stirring quote. Now Jaine couldn't tear her gaze off the hot guy conducting her interview. The blond hair ruffled across his forehead made him resemble a Venice Beach surfer, not the general manager of a family theme park.

Winter sports seemed his thing though, considering the

posters flanking Cinderella. In one, a skier whipped down a powdery slope while the other showed a snowboarder in mid-air. Inspirational words stretched across the bottom of each print: *Goal-Setting* for the skier and *Persistence* for the snowboarder.

To nail this interview, Jaine needed to demonstrate her prowess in both areas. And show that she wasn't some weirdo who talked to herself.

She recovered her voice. "Actually, I'm hoping to help your company find some marketing magic. Uh, thank you for inviting me in." Jaine toed her navy blue dress shoes into the industrial carpet, hoping he didn't notice her fidgeting. When the receptionist had escorted her into the office to wait, she hadn't expected such a good-looking man to join her.

Focus, Jaine. Focus.

"What makes you think Storybook Valley needs marketing magic?" Dylan asked.

Jaine flattened her shoes onto the floor and manufactured a confident smile. "I brought my eight-year-old niece here a few weeks ago and found a crowd small enough to fit into a thimble. You have great attractions—the water park, roller-coaster, and Cinderella's Castle to name a few. But when I brought Amber to one of your competitors, Duke's Animal World, they had double the visitors. They have a nice zoo, but charge extra for train tickets and carnival rides. Storybook Valley's prices are much more reasonable, and your rides are so unique. You're not getting the turnout you deserve."

After her excursion with Amber, Jaine spent two hours crafting a full-page cover letter, fine-tuning and printing out her resume, and selecting writing clips to include in the envelope.

"And you think it relates to marketing? We produced this in the spring." Dylan pushed a glossy tri-fold brochure across the desk.

Although Jaine had read the brochure before, she examined it out of politeness. The front panel depicted tight shots of the flying Glass Slippers, the Ferris wheel, an adorable boy astride a pony, a girl coasting down the water slides, and a family with Cinderella.

"A brochure only helps if it gets into your target audience's hands." She tapped the leaflet with her fingernail. "I've seen those on racks alongside fifty other brochures. You need to take an aggressive approach like strategic billboards, TV ads, and radio contests. Send free passes to newspapers, parenting magazines, and travel editors in the Northeast and invite them to a media weekend. I'll bet a local hotel would offer you a reduced rate because of the publicity opportunity. Don't your relatives own the inn down the street? Paying for meals and accommodations is a miniscule price for the publicity."

Dylan steepled his hands together, expression thoughtful. She guessed he was around twenty-seven or twenty-eight, a couple years older than she was. After submitting her resume, Jaine had anticipated hearing from his father or grandfather. In the few newspaper articles she discovered online, they were the spokesmen. Instead, Dylan had called her.

"Good ideas, only we're tight on money since adding the water park," Dylan said.

"Think of the potential revenue. The media weekend would generate exposure in newspapers, magazines, and online, encouraging thousands of families to visit Storybook Valley. Start with one marketing project and build from there."

"Sounds like you've given these plans lots of thought."

She flipped open the brochure and gestured to the park map. "You have the right ingredients, but some people don't know Storybook Valley exists. Others remember the small park from their childhoods, fun if you're nearby, but not worth traveling state lines. The Catskills is a stellar location and you have quality attractions. Although offering another show or two wouldn't be a bad idea. Families need breaks to calm down cranky kids."

His mouth quirked, whether in amusement or annoyance, she couldn't tell. Did she sound too critical? Jaine needed to remember Dylan's relatives owned the park. He might not appreciate constructive criticism—even though she was right.

"Not only do you have marketing ideas, but you have a plan for improving the attractions," Dylan commented.

His green eyes reflected a faint glint of laughter. She'd just outlined how to increase his family's wealth, and he thought it was funny? Jaine averted her gaze from the longest fringe of lashes she had ever seen on a man. *Focus! You're helping him and hopefully yourself.* Janie squared her shoulders and continued.

"Look, you guys are getting creamed by giraffes and ostriches. Duke's Animal World is taking your customers because they know how to promote themselves. Storybook Valley needs help, or it wouldn't have been dead when Amber and I came during the start of your peak season. Even today, the lot is half-empty."

Jaine spread her portfolio across the desk, forcing Dylan to unlock his hands and slide back in his swivel chair. "Hire me and I'll make this the most popular family attraction in the Northeast."

Crap. Had she really promised that? Jaine clamped her lips shut before any other insane statements slipped out. Dylan didn't speak while he leafed through the plastic-enclosed pages containing her clips and samples. He scanned press releases, company newsletters, and brochures from her last position as a part-time marketing assistant for Mountain View Medical Center. She waited for the inevitable question: if she was so valuable, why didn't she make the cut?

Dylan closed the portfolio and retrieved her resume from one of his piles. "I read about the layoffs. That must have been tough. What was it, forty-five people?"

Jaine dipped her head into a cautious nod. "My supervisor, the marketing director, has been there ten years. They kept her on board, but not me. It was disappointing because she thought my position would evolve into full-time."

"Are you sure promoting Wolf Run won't be too frivolous after educating people about colon cancer screenings, heart surgery advances, and Multiple Sclerosis support groups?" A smile teased the corners of his lips.

He read the newsletter clips she submitted, or at least the headlines, and remembered the details. Would he offer her the job? One that Storybook Valley hadn't advertised or known they needed? How amazing if the owners of the sixty-year-old theme park created a position just for her.

"Are you kidding?" Jaine asked. "Promoting a wooden coaster that plummets from heights of eighty-five feet and races to speeds of fifty-five miles per hour would be a refreshing change of pace."

"You know your stats. Have you ridden Wolf Run?"

"Me? God, no, but I'd enjoy publicizing it. Even though I enjoyed writing about health resources, working for a hospital makes you more aware of illness and disease. Sometimes, it's hard not to dwell on that. I'd love to do marketing for a place where families can spend quality time together. I'd consider it a special honor since I've been coming here since I was little. Storybook Valley has given me lots of happy memories."

Jaine hoped Dylan recognized her sincerity. She couldn't tell what he was thinking as he probed her resume. She'd always tensed entering the hospital's automatic double doors, seeing uneasy people heading to tests, medical procedures, or to visit ailing loved ones. Jaine interviewed staff members and patients for her projects, and while she found the topics informative, her job hadn't been fun.

Jaine could use a dose of pleasure in her life, and merriment was why Storybook Valley existed. When she was a kid, she and her family spent hours riding the canopied train, watching fairy tale characters sing on stage, and snapping pictures with Cinderella. Once, her dad shelled out forty bucks for balloon darts so he could win pink unicorns for his three girls.

She had to convince Dylan that he needed her on his team. Jaine segued into the next topic on her mental checklist. "Have you considered offering an education program for May, June, and October? I'll bet schools would book field trips if there were an educational component. They could choose from different tracks: fairy tales and literature for younger children and science, math, and engineering for older grades. You could keep a handful of rides open and offer them a lunch plan."

"I like how your mind works." Dylan deposited her resume beside a framed picture of a lanky yellow Labrador Retriever with brown eyes so gentle that Jaine longed to rub its soft coat. "Developing an educational curriculum is one of my short-term goals."

"Despite my suggested changes, I wanted to make sure you know that I'm aware how special Storybook Valley is, even down to the courtesy of the staff. During the visit with my niece, the ride attendants were so friendly, opening and closing gates and saying thank you. Even the workers in the gift shops and snack bars asked Amber her favorite rides and recommended attractions."

"That's what I want to hear. Our employee incentive program rewards staff members for small things like that." Dylan groped into a desk drawer and plucked out a sheet of gold star stickers. "Supervisors hand out stars if they notice an employee going above and beyond their duties. They can be redeemed for gift cards, candy, and merchandise. We hold an Employee Rides Night after hours, a Water Park Night, summer cookouts, and an end-of-season Awards Night."

"No wonder the staff seems content. That's wonderful."

"Satisfied employees lead to satisfied guests." Dylan slid the stickers back into his drawer. "So. . .do you see Amber a lot?"

Jaine blinked at the unexpected question. "When I can. We've had more time since I've been unemployed."

Oops, she shouldn't remind him about her job situation. Despite his understanding, everyone knew it looked better if you were employed.

"She's busy with summer camp right now," Jaine added, hoping to distract him. "It's an all-day program."

"You like kids then?" he prodded.

"Sure. Kids are great."

Jaine spent many hours with her niece while her sister, a pharmaceutical company sales rep, peddled women's vitamins and dermatology creams to doctors' offices. Jaine was on a first name basis with moms in the school's parent pickup line and at gymnastics. Amber always thanked her for the chauffeuring and homework help, but Jaine's sister rarely did.

Dylan scrutinized Jaine, arms folded across his royal blue shirt with the Storybook Valley logo stamped over the left in white block letters. "Do you wear contacts?"

"I have plenty of media contacts. Wait. Did you say wear contacts? You mean instead of these?" Jaine fingered the earpiece of her gold-rimmed glasses.

"Right. Contact lenses."

She gave a nervous chuckle. "I scheduled a consultation in college, but was too squeamish to insert the lens. I was more comfortable in glasses."

Was she really justifying her vision enhancement choices to her prospective new boss? Maybe he intended to discuss medical benefits. Or did he think she looked nerdy? What was the saying? Guys don't make passes at girls who wear glasses? Not that she *wanted* him to make a pass even if he *was* hot.

"How blind are you without glasses?" Dylan persisted.

"You wouldn't want to drive with me."

"How about if you're walking around a building? Are you in danger of hurting yourself?"

This interview had taken the Mad Hatter Freeway from Fairy Tale Land into Wonderland where nothing made a damn bit of sense. Did this guy have a glasses fetish, like those weirdoes with shoe fetishes?

"I should be okay. I take them off for special occasions."

8

In fact, Jaine's older sister Bree, who was getting married in August, remarked just last week, "You *are* losing the glasses for my wedding pictures, right?"

What the hell. She'd be a good sport and hope Dylan would be so grateful to pick the brain of a real, flesh and blood, bespectacled person that he would appoint her marketing director. Jaine removed her glasses and the fine details of her surroundings fuzzed. She nodded toward the framed print hanging on a side wall, the picture a wash of symbols and colors. "I can tell that's a park map, but the words and images smear together."

And that was myopia in a nutshell. Jaine adjusted her glasses back into place so she could see his reaction. Dylan examined her with such intensity that a blush stained her cheeks. She patted her French braid, in case stray strands were straggling out.

"Here's the situation," Dylan said. "I took over the general manager position a few months ago. I'm evaluating possible changes and researching how other theme parks run. My grandfather and father have worked with a marketing firm for years to create our brochures, billboards, print, and radio ads."

Jaine's shoulders caved, imperceptible to him, but it felt as if her whole body was sinking.

No fairy tale job ending for her.

"I think we could produce most of those materials in-house," Dylan continued, and her breath bottled up in her chest. "The firm is expensive and I'm not impressed with their efforts. Summer is our busiest season and I'm not ready to implement a full-time marketing position, but I could hire you in that role effective November second, when the park closes and I can devote more time to your training. Most of our positions are seasonal, but the key spots are year-round."

Jaine exhaled. He was offering her a job in her field, promoting a family attraction that once enhanced her childhood. Plus, it gave her an excuse to limit her babysitting availability without guilt. Her sister had received free childcare long enough; she could arrange an alternative.

"Besides the PR and education programs, you'd help to expand our group sales efforts," Dylan went on. "You would invite companies to consider us for their picnics and outings and work with our catering department to make sure the event goes smoothly. Another responsibility would be to promote our new online corporate ticket program where businesses can give discounted tickets to their employees. I'm in the middle of re-designing our website and you'd update content. If everything goes well, there's advancement potential. I foresee expanding the marketing department in a year or two."

An opportunity to shimmy up the corporate beanstalk! Before retirement, her father worked as vice president of an advertising agency, and her over-achiever siblings were always shooting through the ranks of their respective jobs. Now she could latch onto her own chance at success. . .except with her unemployment money running out soon, November seemed far away.

"I'd love to accept your offer." Jaine hesitated. "It's just. . .is it possible to start earlier?"

A hint of a smile slipped across his mouth, contrasting with the furrow grooving his forehead. "I hoped you'd say that. We have a temporary seasonal position that needs filling. It's thirty-five hours per week and I could add on another five hours to spend on marketing. After Labor Day, we'll expand your marketing hours and limit the temporary position to weekends."

Between the furrow and the cautious note in his voice, Jaine was getting a bad feeling, like Hansel and Gretel must have felt when standing before the oven. "What kind of temporary position?"

And how did it involve glasses?

Dylan wheeled his chair around and pointed to the castle poster. She followed his thumb toward the girl in an elegant white and gold gown. "I need a Cinderella."

Chapter Two

Jaine stared at Dylan to gauge whether he was kidding. Oh God, he wasn't kidding. As he lowered his hand, tightness lodged in the pit of her stomach. "Cinderella?"

"Since you've been coming here for so long, you must realize Cinderella is our centerpiece character. She sits on her throne all day, posing for pictures. She leads story times in the castle and appears during our weekend Meet and Greet Fireworks Gala."

"What happened to the regular Cinderella?"

"She didn't work out." He fiddled with the pens poking out of a ski boot-shaped shot glass. "One of my cousins plays the part a couple days per week and fills in when she can, but her schedule doesn't allow her to fulfill our full-time needs. It's the middle of July and I'm tired of fooling around with Cinderella."

He grinned, his dimples diverting her from the princess problem. "That didn't come out right. But you know what I mean. It's getting frustrating, Jaine. I'm having a hard time finding someone reliable."

She bet that Cinderella wouldn't get tired of fooling around with him. Thank goodness, Dylan couldn't peek into the gutter of her mind. What was wrong with her? This was a children's theme park, for heaven's sake.

12

"I can see where you're frustrated, but—"

"Having the position covered for this season would give me plenty of time to find a replacement and a couple backups for next year. Meanwhile, you'd get a behind-the-scenes glimpse of how we operate, which would help with your marketing campaign."

Dylan winked. "Sort of like Cinderella Undercover."

"Were you ever a salesman?" One of her heels tapped against the carpet and she stepped down hard with her other foot to still herself.

"I was a ski instructor and an instructor for an aerial challenge course. Zip lines, tightrope walks, and suspended bridges. I sold beginners on my assurance that I would keep them alive. I wouldn't ask if I didn't think you were capable of pulling it off, Jaine."

She sighed. "I think I would prefer a zip line. I look nothing like a princess. Even without glasses."

Cinderella's hair didn't frizz in the rain, and she would have fit into the snug suit Jaine wanted to wear today. Jaine bet that if Cinderella existed, she'd have silky locks, a body toned from leisurely strolls with her prince, and 20/20 vision that made the entire "Can you walk around without killing yourself?" discussion a moot point.

"Are you serious? I noticed your intelligence when I read your resume and cover letter, but all I saw when you walked into my office was how pretty you are."

Jaine raised her head at his bluntness. Their eyes locked and suddenly the room seemed heated despite the air conditioning.

Dylan suspended his gaze first. "I meant that in a business sense, of course. I've had Cinderella on the brain and I could

13

visualize you in the role."

"Um. . .thank you." Jaine tugged on a wisp of hair and then forced her hand in her lap.

One compliment from a cute guy and she got flustered. It hadn't been that long since a man showed interest in her, right? Oh God, maybe it had been a while, considering the only males she saw on a regular basis were the dads at Amber's gymnastics classes and parent pick-up. Dylan had a position to fill, and here she was more red-faced than a four-teen-year-old whose crush passed her a note in algebra.

"So what does Cinderella do at these Meet and Greet Fireworks?" Jaine asked. "The park didn't have those when I was a kid."

"The characters make a grand entrance on the train. Then they lead a parade around the Castle Cookery pavilion, sign autographs, and dance to a few songs."

"Dance?" Jaine yelped.

She instantly regretted her panicky outburst. Then again, professionalism departed the building five minutes ago.

In a freaking pumpkin coach.

"Just informally with the kids," Dylan said. "Never on stage."

"Dylan—Mr. Callahan—I want to help out, but I can't see myself in this role. Is the year-round position contingent on me saying yes?"

"Call me Dylan. No, of course not, but it would help us out of a jam, and as I mentioned, give you good insider in-formation for future marketing projects." He cleared his throat, his mischievous glint returning. "If you're serious about making Storybook Valley the most popular family at-traction in the Northeast with crowds that won't fit inside a thimble."

I knew I shouldn't have added that stuff.

Why couldn't they need someone to prepare Snow Cones? Fasten seat belts on the Ferris wheel? Sweep popcorn off the pavement? Those chores appealed to her more than three and a half months trapped in a princess costume.

Still, if she cooperated, it should score her brownie points a la mode with whipped cream and a cherry. If Dylan waffled about giving her a raise or expanding her marketing role, she could play the 'Remember-when-I was-such-a-team-player-that-I-let-you-talk-me-into-a-Cinderella-dress' card.

"I expect lots of gold stars for this," Jaine grumbled.

His forehead smoothed and a wide grin showed his relief. "You'll receive plenty. I promise. I'll even buy you a Story-book Valley sweatshirt."

"Hooded, please." Jaine had browsed the sweatshirts on her last visit and recalled that hooded was more expensive.

"Done. I think this is the beginning of a terrific partnership. Welcome to the team." Dylan stood and Jaine admired the tanned legs beneath his black shorts.

He extended his hand. As Jaine shook it, he captured her fingers in his strong grip. Dylan swallowed, and she fought off a tremble. Was he electrified by the physical contact, too?

He's your boss and you want to be taken seriously.

Jaine withdrew her hand, praying her cheeks weren't aflame. "Thank you for the opportunity."

"Thanks for your interest in helping Storybook Valley to grow. Let's get you officially on board."

He led her down the hall into a large office with a dozen desks arranged into low-wall cubicles. Several employees glanced up and smiled at Jaine when she and Dylan passed.

The majority were women from their late teens to early sixties.

"This building is for Human Resources, Finance, IT, and administrative support staff," Dylan told Jaine over his shoulder. "Marketing and Group Sales will be based here, and it's where employees clock in and out. You'll be on a time clock until the end of the season and then we'll put you on salary."

He stopped before an older woman typing on a computer keyboard. Dark hair seasoned with gray bobbed around her ears and a crisp polka dot blouse bloomed over her cranberry capris. She was dressed business casual, unlike Dylan, who wore the same polo shirt and shorts as the ride attendants, food service people, and gift shop personnel.

Dylan's clothes might not be unique, but they fit his athletic body well. Very well.

"Jaine, this is Therese Callahan, my mother. Mom, meet Jaine Andersen, our new jack-of-all-trades." Dylan winked at Jaine and her heartbeat quickened. "Or should we say Jaine-of-all-trades. Mom, could you go over the insurance benefits and have her fill out paperwork? Jaine's signing on as our marketing coordinator and temporary Cinderella. She'll be doing marketing full-time in November."

"We've never had a marketing coordinator. Do your father and grandparents know?" A frown flattened Therese Callahan's pale lips into a straight line.

"They're not making these decisions anymore—I am." Dylan retained more patience than Jaine would have if one of her parents challenged her authority in front of a stranger.

Before her mom died that is. Now, she longed to hear a few more words from her mother, no matter what they were.

"But what about the Ellsworth Agency? We've worked

with them for years. You still plan on using them, don't you?"

"That's under evaluation."

With a sideways look at Jaine, Therese got up and rummaged through a metal file cabinet in the corner. Well, that wasn't the cheerful theme park greeting Jaine expected. A chill pervaded the air, replacing the heat from when she and Dylan were alone. She'd heard that conflict often hampered family-owned businesses, but Jaine imagined that Storybook Valley would be free of that.

Dylan must have noticed her uneasiness. He lowered his voice. "Don't worry. My family isn't fond of change. Soon they'll wonder what they ever did without an in-house marketing coordinator."

"Thanks," she murmured back, hoping he was right.

Through the gingham-curtained windows, Jaine saw the tall white fence that separated the employee section from the rest of the park. This building and the one next door were a pair of charming creamy yellow cottages with gabled rooftops, scalloped gingerbread trim, and powder blue shutters. Further down the way, a third cottage boasted a pink and turquoise color scheme. A sprawling red building with *Food Warehouse* affixed to the side marred the storybook setting, as did the pallets and crates strewn across the pavement and a sideways ladder leaning against the warehouse.

"The other yellow cottage is for Rides, Food Services, Retail, Entertainment, and Security management staff," Dylan said. "The pink one is Wardrobe."

Jaine had never noticed this area behind the fence and doubted that most other guests glimpsed it either unless they happened to peek through the access gate while an employee entered or exited the main park.

Dylan wheeled a swivel chair from an unoccupied desk and signaled for her to sit. "You'll come here for your marketing. Some part-timers leave in the afternoon so you can use an empty cubicle. We'll get a permanent space for you in the fall."

He turned to his mother, who was closing the file cabinet. "I'll radio Krystal. She can work with Jaine tomorrow. Jaine, thanks again for helping us out this summer." He hesitated, as if intending to say something else, and then headed out the door.

Jaine poised on the edge of the chair once she and Therese were left alone.

Therese came back to the desk with a stack of forms, folders, and insurance booklets. She popped a ballpoint pen out of an illustrated Storybook Valley mug on her desk. "Fill out these and then we'll review the insurance. I know you've been hired, and that Dylan has seen your resume, but you still need to complete an employment application. It has information we need on file."

"Of course."

Therese puttered around the office as Jaine jotted her name, address, phone numbers, and email in the appropriate blanks. Jaine paused at the space marked Position Applying For. She wrote Marketing Coordinator and in smaller letters added Temporary Cinderella (through November 2.)

Once she finished outlining her job history, educational background, and provided references, Jaine set aside the application and moved onto the emergency contact sheet.

Lovely. She had to name one of the twins her *in-case-of-emergency*. Which of her sisters would be more likely to arrive at the hospital in a prompt fashion if she. . .got a

18

concussion from being whacked in the head with a camera? Broke her leg dancing?

Bree was balancing wedding planning with her obsessive goal of making partner at her law firm. She'd show up if called, but only after clearing her to-do pile. That left Shauna, who owed her for babysitting but would squeeze in sales visits en route to the hospital.

Therese sat back down and scanned Jaine's application. "Don't you have performing experience? Most of our characters act in community theater or school plays. Several have studied theater in college."

"I'm sorry, but I don't. Dylan didn't ask about that."

"Humph." Therese raised a spiral-bound manual with a purple card stock cover and riffled through the pages. "This is our Character Guide. It stresses how you must *always* stay in character. You don't ask what state a family is from. . .you ask which enchanted land they inhabit. If a boy accompanies his sister to the throne, you don't say, 'Is this your brother?' It's 'Is this your prince?' You'll need a comeback for every personal question."

"Right. Always answer as Cinderella." Jaine nodded, accepting the book that Therese passed to her.

Was it too late to chase after Dylan and demand to know what the hell he had gotten her into?

"You'll have to memorize Cinderella's profile," Therese said. "Be sure to practice her signature until it's a duplicate of the one on page ninety-two. Each character has a personalized signature. Children will see the same familiar handwriting every time they visit. If parents saved autograph books from their own childhoods, they'll find that the signatures haven't changed."

"What amazing attention to detail. That's incredible."

Jaine didn't add that it might go overboard—not all the way down to the Little Mermaid's underwater kingdom, but darn close. Then again, Jaine had applied to the park because of its magical ambiance, which was seeming less magical and more stressful, with each moment.

Therese toyed with the chunky wooden beads on her necklace. "That's what has made our park a success over the decades. My husband's parents started Storybook Valley sixty years ago. They're in their eighties now and still work here. My husband Will recently retired as general manager. He has heart problems, so it was time for him to slow down."

"I'm sorry to hear that."

"He'll be all right if he listens to the doctors—and me—though he's stubborn as the Three Billy Goats Gruff hell-bent on getting past that troll." Therese grimaced. "Dylan took over to keep the park in the family. He's made quite a few changes."

Her voice sounded friendly enough, but Jaine suspected that Therese Callahan could be set in her ways like her husband.

"Now, about our insurance. We use—" Therese broke off as the door swung open.

Little Red Riding Hood whisked into the room, sooty black ringlets spilling out from the satin scarlet hood fastened under her neck. An attached knee-length cape flowed past her lace-up bodice to the hem of her red-and-white-checkered skirt.

Well. *That* was a sight Jaine never saw at Mountain View Medical Center.

"You must be Jaine. I'm Krystal. Also known as, Little Red Riding Hood." She dropped her wicker picnic basket to the floor.

Jaine guessed Krystal was a couple years younger than she was, perhaps twenty-three or twenty-four, unless the light freckles dusting her nose and cheeks just made her appear youthful.

"You look amazing," Jaine marveled. "The exact way I picture Little Red Riding Hood."

"Krystal's been playing Little Red for years," Therese told her. "She's also our wardrobe supervisor. Jaine is our new Cinderella."

Hey, what about marketing coordinator?

"Wow, we're finally seeing an end to the Cinderella Curse?" Krystal asked.

Therese sent Krystal a warning look. "She starts tomorrow. Could you come in a couple hours early and help her to get ready? She needs to learn about her duties at the castle and at the Meet and Greets. I'll have Lois drop by to go over animation."

Animation? Cinderella Curse?

"I expect that you'll memorize Cinderella's profile tonight and practice the signature until it's perfect," Therese continued with an equally stern glance at Jaine. "You'll be tested before you're officially approved for Cinderella. That's our policy regardless of what Dylan told you."

Ouch. Jaine wondered how Dylan would respond to that comment.

"I'll start preparing the moment I get home," Jaine assured her.

This was really happening. Even if she mastered the signature and recited the guidebook, how would any children accept that she was a beautiful princess? No one would call

21

Jaine glamorous. Cute maybe, but not nearly as adorable as Krystal. Anyway, Cinderella wasn't a mere 'cute.' Everyone knew she was breathtaking.

Even three-year-olds.

***

Jaine cringed at her reflection in the wall-to-wall mirrors of the bridal shop fitting room. After her meeting with Therese, Jaine rushed home to her apartment and changed into shorts, then drove to meet her sisters for the scheduled appointment. She stayed positive on the ride to the boutique, hoping the bridesmaid dress color would be less garish in person than on the website.

She needed a fairy godmother to grant that wish. Jaine slinked away from the mirror.

"I love the hot pink. Don't you?" enthused her older sister Bree, the bride-to-be.

"It's eye-catching." Jaine avoided a direct answer while she awaited her turn with the seamstress.

Back in May, Jaine tried on the elegant Venetian Gold floor model. Even though the ruffles cascading in a vertical line down the right side hadn't thrilled her, overall she felt classy in the strapless empire-waisted gown. Unfortunately, Bree insisted on Tutti Frutti, a proper hue for nail polish perhaps, but a full-length gown?

Bree had handed out swatches so the bridesmaids could have their shoes dyed the same shade. Surprisingly, she allowed them to choose their own shoe store and style, as long as the result wound up in Tutti Frutti.

The grandmotherly seamstress finished with Bree's identical twin sister, Shauna, crossed the plush mauve carpet to Jaine, and zipped the gown in an efficient glide. Jaine had struggled to manage the task herself in one of the curtained dressing rooms lining the back wall and finally admitted defeat.

"This is so exciting. I can't believe the wedding is in less than a month and a half." Shauna hugged Bree.

Not for the first time, a thorn of envy prickled inside Jaine. She'd always been odd-one out, the tagalong kid sister. Not only were they fortunate enough to enter the world together, best friends for life, Sabreena and Shauna lucked out on the name front.

Unlike her, named after her spinster great aunt Jane who insisted that the new baby have an *i* in the middle so she wouldn't be a "plain Jane." A nice sentiment, but the spelling had befuddled teachers, Girl Scout troop leaders, doctors' offices, and this bridal shop. Most people forgot the i or pronounced it Janie.

The twins separated and flipped their fine golden hair over their shoulders. Either could play Cinderella with ease though at times their behavior mimicked the bratty stepsisters. Particularly Bree.

"The dress looks nice on you, Jaine," Shauna said.

Had the gaudiness impaired her eyesight, like when you stared at the sun too long?

"Thanks, you too," Jaine responded.

It wasn't a total lie. If anyone could pull off a gown in a teenybopper lip balm shade, it was Shauna.

"Thanks." Shauna fastened the sash on her daughter Amber's taffeta flower girl dress, while Bree appraised Jaine with her courtroom stare, honed by hours of cross-examining witnesses.

Finally, Bree spoke. "I like the dress on you, too."

Okay, if the twins suffered such obvious vision problems, why was Jaine the only sibling in spectacles?

"I'm glad." Jaine supposed that was the most important thing, the bride not regretting the color scheme.

Bree changed the subject. "I noticed that you checked off 'and guest' on your invitation card. I thought you weren't dating anyone."

Jaine stood statue-still as the seamstress tugged gently on the fabric to judge whether it needed taking in. "I'm not."

"Are you bringing a friend? You better warn him that you'll be at the head table and he'll be eating with strangers."

"Who would you ask?" Shauna bunched Amber's chestnut curls into a mound then twisted it into a sideways ponytail, experimenting with flower girl hairstyles.

Amber broke away and pirouetted, doing her best to swirl the taffeta.

"I don't know yet," Jaine answered. "I figured I might meet someone by then."

Not likely, but a girl could wish, right?

"I hope you don't waste the meal," Bree interjected. "Surf and Turf isn't cheap."

"Neither is this dress," Jaine replied sharply.

She cast an apologetic glance at the seamstress who stooped to pin the hem. The woman smirked. At least someone was enjoying this exchange.

Bree rolled her eyes. "You don't have to get sensitive. Of course, I hope you find a date. All I'm saying is if you don't, please give me a heads-up."

"It might be hard to meet someone in time," Shauna said.

"Since you're not working, I mean."

"Actually, I'm the new marketing coordinator at Storybook Valley." Jaine allowed herself a small boast. "They created the position for me after I mailed a blind resume."

She skipped the Cinderella thing. Boy, would her sisters— and the seamstress—chuckle over that little tidbit. In the twins' case, guffaw.

"That's great, but does this mean you won't be able to mind Amber after school?" Shauna bit down on her glossy lower lip as her daughter spun before a mirror across the room. "Or pick her up from summer camp on days that I work late?"

"I'm sorry, Shauna, but you knew I would find a full-time job eventually." Jaine's stomach sank at the worried expression inching across Shauna's attractive face.

Don't feel guilty. Amber was her niece, not her daughter, and she needed to earn a living. Shauna never paid her for babysitting or reimbursed her for the Kraft mac and cheese, frozen chicken nuggets, and Goldfish crackers that Jaine stocked in her apartment. Jaine adored her niece, but watching her didn't pay the bills.

"It's just. . .now I'll have to find a good after-school program, arrange busing, and rearrange her gymnastics schedule." Shauna splayed a hand across her throat, gleaming ivory-tipped fingernails blending in with her string of pearls. "Jaine, can you research after-school places and tell me which ones look best? If you screen the web sites first that will save so much time."

Jaine's shoulders slumped. She had plenty of her own tasks to handle, but Shauna had worked hard to become one of her company's top pharmaceutical reps. She raised Amber alone with no help from her loser ex-husband. Jaine would be busy with the theme park, but she wasn't juggling single parent-hood.

"Okay, I'll look into it, but not this week. Let me get comfortable at Storybook Valley first."

"Thanks, Jaine! I can always rely on you." Shauna flashed her a relieved smile.

"So you really took a job at that old amusement park? I thought just high school kids worked there." Bree pivoted toward the mirror and brushed an invisible speck off her tailored olive pantsuit.

"Of course not," Jaine said. "They have professional positions, like any other big business. How else would the park run?"

"Still, I'm surprised they can afford a marketing coordinator," Shauna commented. "Amber went to a birthday there last year, and it was a ghost town."

Jaine tuned out her sisters, distracted by a new worry. Her job offer unfolded so quickly that she forgot to request time off for the bachelorette party, rehearsal, and wedding.

Maybe the bachelorette party was pushing it. The event was a couple weeks away. She'd better skip the restaurant and just show up at the club after the fireworks. Since she dreaded dealing with Bree's wrath, Jaine would save that revelation for another day.

After the seamstress unzipped her again, Jaine ducked into a dressing room to change. Once she was back in her regular clothes, she scanned her reflection in the mirror inside her stall.

What possessed Dylan to cast her as Cinderella? Shoulder-length waves fell around Jaine's oval face. Bree used to say that Jaine's hair couldn't decide whether it was blonde or brown. Jaine preferred the term "sandy," but even that wasn't entirely correct. Outside, sun captured the gold highlights, but indoors the color leaned toward caramel.

Jaine didn't dislike her hair, but it wasn't anything special, nor were her blue eyes. Even with mascara, they didn't pop from behind her glasses. When Shauna tried talking her into the sexy librarian look, Jaine couldn't persuade herself to buy the bold, black cat eye frames, instead opting for subtle gold.

She still hadn't found lipstick that plumped out her thin lips, but Jaine used a pale pink shade that helped slightly. Oh well. Jaine draped her handbag over her shoulder. Her transformation into Cinderella was Krystal's problem.

She joined her sisters and niece in the showroom where mannequins in wedding gowns and bridesmaid dresses occupied the front window.

"What's everyone doing tonight?" Jaine asked as they strolled to the parking lot. "Anyone want to grab dinner?"

"Can't, I'm heading to the office." Bree perused the texts on her cell phone. "We're prepping for a big case, and I've got to email the other girls and remind them to schedule their fittings."

"Amber's having a slumber party. Lots of popcorn and S'mores right, Amber?" In her stylish blazer and skirt set, Shauna looked ready for a business meeting rather than a sleepover.

Amber bounced along beside her mother. "Yep, and pancakes for breakfast."

Bree wrinkled her nose. "Giggling girls and cooking. Have fun, sis."

"Working all night? Ugh," Shauna retorted.

Despite their opposite life paths, with Bree graduating at the top of her law school class and settling down in her late twenties and Shauna raising a child as a divorced single mom, the twins maintained their childhood bond. And Jaine kept hers as the third wheel.

Bree kissed both her sisters on the cheek. "Thanks for coming, ladies. Good luck with the job, Jaine, and have fun tonight, kiddo." She slapped Amber a high-five.

"Good luck, Jaine," Shauna echoed. "Hope it's perfect for you."

Amber walked backwards to face her aunt. "Hey, Aunt Jaine? Next time I'm at the park, can you get me extra time with Cinderella?"

Chapter Three

Jaine jolted awake to the static grumble of the alarm clock and the sandpapery tickle of her cat, Willow, lapping up her ear.

"I'll feed you in two minutes," Jaine mumbled, curling onto her side.

Awareness penetrated her brain fog. She had stayed up until 2 a.m. reviewing the employee handbook, memorizing the character profile, and writing "Cinderella" in fancy curlicue script until her hand cramped. Today she had to wear a ball gown and brave the mysterious Cinderella Curse.

Arghhhhhhhhh.

Jaine burrowed under her covers, Willow purring beside her and kneading the patchwork quilt with black paws.

If only she could stay home with her cat. She had adopted Willow from the shelter last year after her father married Gloria and sold the house. Jaine grew up in a restored 1920s farmhouse overlooking a four-acre backyard and serene mountain landscape. She spent countless evenings reading on the porch, creaking in the maple rocking chair, the fragrance of wildflowers filtering through the screens. On cool nights she zipped her favorite sweatshirt or huddled under a fleecy blanket.

Now all that remained from those peaceful evenings was

the chair hulking in a corner of her bedroom under a laundry pile.

Jaine threaded her fingers through her cat's fur. Although she preferred to hide out, the real world awaited in the guise of a princess castle.

She showered, dressed, and picked at a few bites of toast and melon. Jaine released her pent-up breath. Time to drive her chariot to the kingdom.

The familiar ride to work soothed her nerves. Jaine knew these rolling farmlands, quaint antique shops, and tree-fringed streets. She'd grown up here. Summer delivered an influx of tourists from New York City, but this early in the morning, it didn't affect traffic.

When Jaine arrived at Storybook Valley, she pulled into the employee lot beside a dozen other cars with matching parking decals in the windshield. Krystal waved from the high brown fence that lined the park's perimeter, a canvas bag slung over her shoulder and a peach sundress showing off her slim figure.

Jaine bypassed the covered alleys where guests would purchase tickets and have their hands stamped and joined Krystal at a gate bearing the sign *Employees Only*.

"Hey! Ready to be fairy-godmotherized?" Krystal asked, unlatching the gate.

"I guess so."

"You don't sound too sure. We'll clock in first, and then I'd better get you to Wardrobe before you change your mind."

Beyond the fence, a groundskeeper pushed a lawnmower across the glittering grass and a couple of teenage girls carried brooms and dustpans down a gravel walkway. In the background, the lush green Catskills painted the landscape.

"I didn't realize employees worked this early," Jaine said as they passed a garden decked out with grubby bearded ceramic gnomes.

"Grounds and maintenance are always the first ones here and last to leave. The characters arrive forty-five minutes to an hour before their shift to get into costume and makeup, and then Rides and Foods show up for their morning meeting. Dylan's usually here early, too."

Dylan, huh? Jaine wouldn't mind running into her attractive boss assuming it preceded her Cinderella transformation.

She and Krystal ambled by the Puss in Boots Corn Maze, a kiddie labyrinth crafted out of artificial cornstalks. At the maze's exit awaited a feline statue in a plumed hat, cape, and lofty boots. Jaine trailed Krystal down a "street" of life-sized dioramas, housing Animatronic figures from fairy and folk tales. Amber loved the Princess and the Pea exhibit, depicting a girl dozing atop a stack of covered mattresses and a mechanical breathing dog napping on the floor.

"They must have everyone doing double duty around here if you're the wardrobe supervisor and Little Red Riding Hood."

"Not really. When they promoted me, after I graduated from cosmetology school, I asked if I could keep dressing up. It's Halloween every day when you wear a costume."

"But since you're in the wardrobe department you don't get to interact with the kids, do you?" Jaine asked.

"I walk around a couple times per day to give autographs and I do the weekend Meet and Greets. Those are the best."

A supervisor who preferred a cape and hood to her own clothes. Okaaay.

"I heard Cinderella is just a short-term thing for you

31

though." Krystal shot Jaine a look. "I can see why Dylan corralled you into playing her. You've got a sweetness to you."

Sweetness? Wasn't glamorous the quality that girls sought in a princess? And in that department, Jaine was lacking.

Once they reached the partitioned-off employee area, Jaine checked her hair in the window before entering the bungalow where she'd had her interview. Following Krystal's instructions, she flashed her time card under the scanner.

"Rides Night is this Friday." Krystal gestured to a flyer tacked to a large bulletin board. "After the park closes, they'll keep a couple rides open and grill hotdogs for the employees."

Finally, a fun perk of working for a theme park. It would have excited Jaine more if she wasn't making the walk of shame toward the Cinderella costume. They left the bungalow and she trailed Krystal past an employee bike rack, a golf cart, and a truck stuffed with white garbage bags. They stopped before the third gabled cottage in the lot, soft pink with turquoise shutters.

As Krystal unlocked the door and flicked on the light, Jaine blinked at the row of disembodied heads leering from a suspended rack. The upside down faces of the Gingerbread Man, the park's mascot Dazzle the Dragon, the Frog King, and a giant fox appeared gruesome without bodies attached.

"That's our Wall of Heads," Krystal said. "Creepy, huh? It's even spookier at night."

"I can imagine." Jaine studied a long rack of hanging fairy tale costumes. She recognized the fairy godmother gown and Cinderella's dress. They had several duplicates of each costume, probably in different sizes. That reminded her. . .

"I've got to know. What's the Cinderella Curse?"

"Oh, that." Krystal dropped her voice even though they were alone. "We've had problems with the last few Cinderellas."

"What kind of problems?"

"I'll tell you while I do your makeup." Krystal escorted her over to a long table and mirror that ran along an entire wall.

She scraped out two metal chairs, gestured for Jaine to sit, and spread her supplies across the counter. "We'll issue a bunch of products to you. I'll write down everything I'm doing. Soon you'll be able to get ready without me."

Jaine nodded, more interested in the Cinderella Curse than the Cinderella Makeover that would disappoint her with its lackluster results. She removed her prescription sunglasses and slipped them back into her handbag alongside her regular glasses.

Krystal squirted a creamy white base onto her fingertip and rubbed it over Jaine's eyelids. "Avery had the job last year. She acted normal until this past Memorial Day weekend. She showed up at the castle with purple hair, Goth makeup, black boots, and a spider web tattoo on her arm."

"Tell me she wasn't wearing the Cinderella costume."

"Not only did that fruitcake wear it, but she lectured a bunch of preschoolers about how fairy tale princesses set unfair beauty standards and how children need to show society they're not putting up with this crap. That's a direct quote."

"Are you kidding me? She told that to kids?"

Krystal penciled a brown tint beneath Jaine's lower lashes. "I swear on my paycheck. According to legend, her boyfriend dumped her for a lingerie model and she snapped."

"I'll say."

"Parents went ballistic and stormed Guest Relations," Krystal continued, penciling Jaine's other eye. "Dylan fired her, refunded the money of every family that witnessed the ordeal, and gave out free passes. Since then, we've had a new rule that characters need my approval before they report to their locations. If I'm not here, they have to pop into the front office and see Therese or Dylan. He was irked we didn't have that policy all along, but nothing like this had ever happened."

"That's too bad." Jaine tried to ignore the uncomfortable tickling sensation underneath her eye. "Avery had a point about the standards, but you don't go out on a rampage at your job. That explains why Dylan wants to be careful."

"He thought he was being careful with Cinderella Number Two."

"Uh oh."

"Dylan promoted a girl from within the park, a high school senior who worked in one of the snack bars. She was a National Honor Society student, class president, and yearbook editor, so she seemed ideal."

"She wasn't?" Jaine did a silent cheer when Krystal finished with the eyeliner.

"Nope, she was *too* qualified. The girl got offered a long term office temp job and gave us a day's notice."

"Yikes."

"Exactly." Krystal flipped open a compact in two complementary hues of eye shadow. She brushed mint green across Jaine's lids and added a few darker strokes in the inner creases. "That brings us to the last Cinderella. Regan. Dylan hired the sister of a friend. Regan was a nice girl entering her junior year of college."

"But?"

"She got herself knocked up, had a vicious case of morning sickness, and puked her guts out during story time. A couple kids hurled from the odor. People flew out of the castle so fast that you'd think Dazzle the Dragon was spitting fire behind them." Krystal grasped an eyelash curler like scissors.

"No way! Oh, Krystal! That's awful!" Jaine shuddered, partly from the menacing strip hovering over the root of her lashes.

"Close your eye. . .there, now open it," Krystal ordered. "Tell me if I pinch the skin."

Pinch? Tickling had been bad enough. Jaine sat frozen as Krystal closed the curler over her lashes, squeezed lightly, and turned it upward. What insane ritual was this? Jaine had heard of eyelash curlers, in the same abstract way she had heard of bikini waxing, but she'd never used one. Sure, she wore makeup, but Jaine spent five minutes on a simple routine of lip gloss, blush, a few dabs of eye shadow, and if she was going out at night, mascara. Nothing this intricate.

"We couldn't have a Cinderella with a royal bun in the oven even if she wasn't projectile vomiting." Krystal released the handles in small pulses with light pressure.

This curling craziness didn't hurt, but Jaine wouldn't call it comfortable either. At least she had the Cinderella gossip to distract her.

"Dylan transferred her to the gift shop and was searching for a replacement when you came along," Krystal continued. "Don't blink, okay?"

No wonder Dylan grew tired of fooling around with Cinderella. The turnover would have frustrated Jaine, too.

Her other eyelid fluttered in sympathy for its poor, trapped

35

partner in vision. Krystal walked the curler up from the root of the lash to the tip, pressing and pulsing.

"Goth Princess, Too Big for Her Britches Princess, and Puke Princess," Jaine said. "The Cinderella Curse. If I throw in the tiara, Dylan will hate me forever."

"Yep. This is his first full season taking over, and he's stressed out enough. That new water park should spray diamonds for what it cost and we're not seeing much increase in business." Krystal opened the curler, examined her handiwork, nodded, and moved on to the second set of skinny lashes.

Once she had completed the curling, Krystal drew out tweezers. Jaine shied away. "What are you doing with those?"

"No offense, but you need plucking." Krystal cupped Jaine's face and tilted it back to center.

"Ow!" Jaine winced as the determined wardrobe supervisor tugged at a hair on the outside of her brow, wielding the pincers with too much enthusiasm. She yanked another hair and then another.

By the time Krystal finished, Jaine's eyes watered and her nose itched. Jaine had plucked now and then, but she'd slacked off during her period of unemployment. And she'd never been this thorough.

"Much better. Wow, I'm good. Damn good." Krystal stared at her for a moment and then fumbled in her case for more tools.

Over the next few minutes, Krystal added mascara, powder, blush, lip liner, and lipstick. With each new cosmetic, Jaine's curiosity intensified. Even Bree on her wedding day wouldn't receive this much pampering. Her sister was hiring someone for nails and hair, but not this other stuff.

"First, you'll put on the dress, then we'll do the wig," Krystal said once she had finished. "You've got to see yourself though."

Jaine glanced into the mirror above the makeup table. Her lips—her full, lustrous lips—parted as her mouth dropped open. Whoa! And her beautiful eyes! Normally her long thin lashes jutted straight out, but they had thickened into inky fullness, making her eyes seem bigger. Her brows had a soft, angled appearance that enhanced her oval face shape.

"You're an absolute knockout." Krystal gave an approving nod.

"And you're amazing. You could be a Hollywood makeup artist. Thank you so much for spending all this time on me." Jaine couldn't rip her gaze from the mirror.

"We're not done yet." Krystal slid hangers along the bar of the costume rack, fabric rustling. She lingered at the ball gowns and inspected the tags in the collar. She unhooked one and rested it against her arm, still on the hanger. Gleaming pearls and silver thread embroidered the layers of rich gold.

"I think the size six will be a good fit for you. The Callahans had the costume designed, based on the dress described in Charles Perrault's retelling of Cinderella. They're committed to authenticity here. You'll have three costumes—one to wear, one for backup, and one for cleaning. Each one has a label so we can keep track of them. Include the code, your name, and the time on the clipboard near the door. After your shift, hang the gown on the laundry rack."

Krystal nodded toward a wheeled cart against the back wall, brimming with costumes. "We have wardrobe clerks that help with laundry and sewing. If your costume ever needs mending, let us know. Come on. I'll show you where to change."

Krystal shuttled the gown down a short corridor that ended with two doors, marked Men's and Women's Locker Rooms.

The women's room reminded Jaine of high school gym class with its curtained dressing stalls and gray lockers. Krystal handed her a combination lock along with a slip bearing the numbers.

"Okay, Cinderella, do you want help getting into the dress?"

"I think I can handle it."

Krystal peeled back a curtain and suspended the gown onto a hook. "Meet you in the Costume Shop."

Left alone with her gown, Jaine surveyed it from top to bottom. The wardrobe gods wouldn't give her a happy medium. First the don't-look-at-it-too-long-or-you'll-go-blind bridesmaid dress, now a ball gown so puffy that helium could have inflated it. Like Goldilocks, she yearned for something just right.

Jaine stripped off her shirt and shorts, climbed into the gown with its tulle petticoat, and yanked up the back zipper. A little tight, but out of all her complaints about this costume, the fit ranked dead last. Her resemblance to a parade float, well, that was the bigger issue.

She patted the middle, attempting to tame the tulle, and shuffled bare-footed into the Costume Shop.

Krystal clapped. "Magnificent!"

Jaine had to admit, it was gorgeous in the frilly way little girls adored. She suspected that it cost more than any garment she owned, including her bridesmaid gown. When she was a child, she would have loved playing dress-up in this outfit.

Now as an adult? Not so much.

"Time for the wig," Krystal announced.

Ugh. Jaine had forgotten that part.

Within minutes, Krystal was separating Jaine's hair into pieces, twisting and clipping it into place. She pulled a cap around Jaine's ears and then removed a fluffy blonde up-sweep wig from a Styrofoam head. She slipped it onto Jaine from front to back.

"This is a classic Gibson Girl style." Krystal adjusted a silver tiara around the bun. "You might find the wig itchy at first, but you'll get used to it. After this, we'll go over to the castle and you'll spend a half hour with Lois Callahan, Dylan's grandmother. She'll work with you on the performance aspects of being Cinderella."

Krystal chose a pair of translucent pumps from the cubbies beneath the costume rack. "If these don't work, we have a couple other sizes."

Jaine pressed her feet into the "glass" slippers and wiggled her toes. "They seem okay. I'll walk to be sure."

She got up and wandered in a circle. The shoes had a slight heel, but nothing she couldn't manage. Krystal motioned toward the full-length mirror. "What do you think?"

Squinting at her reflection, Jaine edged closer. Even without glasses, she saw that once again, Krystal had performed a miracle. Jaine assumed the wig would look fake, but somehow it appeared natural. Curls rolled over her forehead and bounced along both sides of her neck.

"You're really blind, aren't you?" Krystal asked with a laugh. "One more inch and you'll bump into the mirror. Goth Princess had a point. If Harry Potter can wear spectacles why can't Cinderella?"

As Jaine observed herself in the tiara and ball gown, a memory poured over her.

Her mother helped Jaine into a sparkling pink costume in the Storybook Valley gift shop. Jaine clutched a plastic wand with a light-up star at the top. "Look at me, I'm a real princess!" Jaine exclaimed. "Can we buy it?"

Her mother enclosed her in a warm hug. "Yes, it fits you perfect. But remember that you're my princess even when you're not wearing a fancy dress."

Jaine swallowed around a lump in her windpipe. Hot gumminess slicked her powdered eyelids. Hands gripping each other, she pivoted from the mirror.

"Jaine, are you okay?" Krystal asked. "What's wrong?"

"It's. . . ." Jaine halted her speech to regain control. "I was thinking about my mom and a visit to Storybook Valley. We came at least twice a year. I loved taking pictures with Cinderella and once my mom bought me a princess costume to wear in the picture. She. . .she died a few years ago."

Krystal foraged into her bag and found a package of tissues. Jaine accepted one for her runny nose.

"I'm sorry, Jaine. That must be so hard to have a close relationship with your mother and then lose her."

"It is. I'm close to my dad, too, but haven't seen him much since he remarried and moved to Florida." She didn't tell Krystal how much her father's absence stung.

Jaine crumpled the damp tissue into the wastebasket and pressed the heel of her palm against the heaviness in her chest. "Mom would have laughed at this Cinderella gig. She was always telling me to loosen up. Her nagging used to get on my nerves. Now I wish she was here to nag me."

Her eyes glassy, Krystal linked arms with Jaine. "I know

this won't help, but I lost my mother when I was three and barely remember her. Even though life wasn't fair to you either, treasure the time you had together. Not everyone gets that."

Krystal was right. How different Jaine's life would have been if she hadn't shared those precious years with her mother. Birthdays, holidays, and vacations. All the days her mom volunteered at school functions and chaperoned field trips. The nights her mother read stories, and they chatted about Jaine's friends and teachers.

"Thank you, Krystal. I needed to hear that." Jaine squeezed her new friend's hand. "I'm so sorry you grew up without a mother."

"Honestly, I'm crying for your mom, not mine." Krystal hugged her and stepped back. "Believe me, I was better off not having her for my role model, but I wish things had been different."

Jaine pondered that while Krystal changed into her Little Red Riding Hood outfit. Maybe Krystal would confide more once they knew each other better.

Once Krystal emerged from the dressing room, they exited the employee gate behind blue-shirted employees with walkie-talkies and Storybook Valley fanny packs. Jolly music floated through the air as someone switched on a whimsical loop of amusement park tunes.

A teenage girl waved from the control panel beside Wolf Run. "Hey, Red. Hey Cindy!" she called.

Her partner, a college-aged boy, lifted his head from a box of paperwork. "Is that another new Cindy?"

"Maybe I should mention the employee nickname for Cinderella," Krystal told Jaine, waving back.

In this outfit, she would rather have people call her Cindy than recognize her as Jaine. Scents of yeasty donuts sizzling in oil and warm gingerbread cookies baking in the oven wafted from the Little Red Hen Bakery. The aroma enticed Jaine when she visited with Amber, but today the smells unsettled her stomach. She was a storybook character on the outside even if she didn't feel like one on the inside. What if the kids figured out she was a fraud?

Jaine's shoes clicking against the pavement, she matched pace with Krystal. The "slippers" fit tighter than she'd thought. Jaine prayed she'd make it throughout the day without blistering. Or barfing.

If she avoided retching, at least she'd be an improvement on the last Cinderella.

"Home sweet home," Krystal remarked, passing the log cabin of Little Red Riding Hood's grandmother. Across from the house, a tree bore a painted sign with the warning *Beware of Wolf*.

"Let me think, what else can I tell you? You'll lead story times at 10:30 a.m. and 4 p.m. You'll find a bookcase in the castle with all kinds of fairy tales and folk tales, not just famous ones. The Callahans broaden kids' horizons beyond Snow White and Cinderella."

Krystal commented how Jaine was lucky the castle had a small bathroom hidden inside, not that the toilet had done much good for Puke Princess, who hadn't made it there in time.

"If you need to use it, hang a 'Be right back' sign on the castle door. There's another sign for your breaks with an adjustable clock attached. Most employees aren't allowed to eat at their location, but there's an exception for Cinderella.

When she wanders around the park it attracts attention. We're not large enough to have a greeter assigned to you all day, but if you want to leave the castle, call for help on the walkie-talkie. Someone will escort you back and forth and tell families that Cinderella has to meet Prince Charming. That way you can stay in character and don't have to be a snob, declining pictures."

She gestured toward the insulated bag in Jaine's hand. "You can't carry your lunch around once the park opens or be seen buying food. If you want to buy, arrange to have someone pick up your order."

Krystal rattled on about refrigerator locations, lockers, and food discounts. Jaine nodded absently, eyeing the grey stone turrets with gold filigree rising through the trees.

How was it possible that she was more nervous than when she'd started at the hospital? High school and college girls worked as Cinderella.

But for those girls, it was a summer job. Jaine had more at stake than the Cinderella gig. By proving herself a team player, she could build a real career here. Jaine looked the part of Cinderella, but now she needed to act like her.

They embarked up the hilly gravel path toward their destination. As if sensing Jaine's preoccupation, Krystal quieted until they reached the castle. Golden pumpkin coaches flanked the archway, a favorite photo spot. Children could clamber inside and peek out open-air windows though the coaches remained stationary. That didn't stop Jaine from wishing a pumpkin would cart her away.

Enchanting instrumental music piped through the sound system. Jaine's hands fidgeted at her sides. "I have this feeling I'm not in Kansas anymore."

"That was Dorothy, honey." Krystal squeezed her shoulder. "You're more like Glinda the Good Witch. Little girls will worship you and boys will want to marry you."

After a long drought on the career and dating front, Jaine was in-demand, albeit among five-year-olds.

She supposed it was better than nothing.

Chapter Four

Jaine waved for what seemed like the hundredth time in ten minutes. She'd better master this princess wave soon, or else she'd be fighting a massive case of carpal tunnel. "Is this better, Mrs. Callahan?"

Lois Callahan shook her head, readjusting Jaine's hand with surprising strength for such a slender woman. Dark blonde hair framed her face in layers and rose blush climbed the apples of her lined cheeks. Her violet silk shirt, sheer jacket, and tailored pants looked straight out of an elegant Manhattan boutique.

"No, my dear, it's elbow, elbow, wrist, wrist. I perfected it for my princess wave when I was Cinderella sixty years ago. Since then I've taught all our Cinderellas to wave the same way."

"Sorry, I'll keep trying." Jaine fluttered her hand yet again while she stood before Lois on the faux marble floor.

Krystal had introduced Lois as the Entertainment Director and mouthed "Good luck" before escaping the castle. First, Lois tested Jaine on her autograph skills, making her redo the flourish on the C ten times before deeming it passable. Next, she quizzed Jaine about Cinderella's extensive background and demonstrated a proper curtsy. Then she rambled about animation—enhancing her role through non-verbal techniques.

"Pretend you're screwing in a light bulb when you're waving," Lois urged, a frustrated note tingeing her refined voice. "Have you ever done that, darling? Screwed in a light bulb?"

"Well, yes, but—"

"Gram, the park's about to open," Dylan interrupted from the doorway. "Why don't you give Jaine a few minutes to relax?"

Terrific. Not only was Jaine's handsome boss seeing her dressed-up as if she were trick or treating, but he had also overheard his grandmother's criticism.

"But we haven't even discussed posture or stage presence. How can she be ready to perform? Look at her shoulders for heaven's sake." Lois swept a regal arm toward Jaine, her finger boasting a vintage carved cameo ring.

What was the matter with her posture? Jaine straightened her spine, wondering if she would ever satisfy Lois Callahan. Dylan's amused eyes met Jaine's exasperated ones.

"Her shoulders are fine. Hey, Gram, could you do me a big favor? We have a new girl giving boat tours and she needs to liven up her speech. How about giving her some tips?"

"Of course, my dear. I hope she has a sense of humor. Passengers love hearing a well-delivered joke."

"There's no one better than you to coach her on technique."

"True." With a sage nod, Lois glanced back at Jaine. "We'll continue with your training another time, darling. For now, do your best. And I must admit you are lovely. Isn't she fetching, Dylan?"

"Very fetching," he agreed.

Okay, maybe Lois Callahan wasn't as overbearing as Jaine thought. She liked the subtle way Dylan re-directed his grandmother though Jaine pitied the poor boat ride operator.

"However, princesses *should* have pearly white teeth. I would suggest extra brushing with my secret ingredients. Lemon and baking soda."

"Gram." Dylan used a warning voice.

"Enjoy your day at the palace, my dear." Lois strolled out the arched front entrance into the humidity, leaving behind a whiff of floral perfume.

"Oh, God," Jaine groaned. "Is she saying I have yellow teeth?"

"The woman has cataracts. Trust me, you're fine."

Even assuming her teeth were acceptable, how would she ever belong in these elegant surroundings? Sparkling chandeliers and crystal wall sconces glowed over the burgundy walls and the impressive tapestries illustrating the Cinderella story. Until her late night study session, Jaine had never realized there had been over seven hundred versions of Cinderella including a 1634 story published in Naples by Giambattista Basile that referred to her as Zezolla. She'd been Rashin Coatie in Scotland, the Flowerpot Princess in Japan, and Cenerentola in Italy, but Charles Perrault created the most famous retelling in 1697. He invented the fairy godmother, pumpkin coach, and glass slipper.

After all her times visiting this castle as a little girl who would have believed that she would be crowned Cinderella, the next in line to uphold centuries of traditions?

Jaine grew aware of Dylan's lingering gaze and her stomach flipped. "I don't know whether to banish you from my palace for getting me into this, or thank you for rescuing me from your grandmother."

"If you banish me, then I can't come back later to give

you gold stars. By the way, thanks for putting up with her. My granddad is a train engineer and my grandmother likes to work with the entertainment staff." The corners of his lips twitched. "They don't always like working with *her*."

At least Jaine wasn't the only one flummoxed by Lois. Still, she admired Lois Callahan's pride in her family business. The real world faded whenever Jaine entered the Storybook Valley gates as a child, perhaps because Lois demanded excellence.

"That's nice you keep your grandparents involved. I'm sure it means a lot to them."

"They're the ones who started all this. But no one can live up to her standards. If Miss America walked in here, my grandmother would critique her stage presence, too."

Jaine released a breath she hadn't realized she'd been holding. "That's good to know. I was feeling unqualified."

"Don't worry. You'll do great. Come on, Your Highness." Dylan ushered her to the throne, his hand brushing against her lower back.

Jaine's stomach gave another flip. They halted before the brass-armed chair but neither moved. She inhaled the crisp scent of Dylan's cologne; it smelled like the outdoors, fresh and woodsy. Was her heart galloping faster than a royal steed because of Dylan's nearness or the park opening?

"Thanks for checking on me," she said.

Finally, almost reluctantly, he lowered his arm and Jaine sank onto the throne. "No problem. Good luck."

Dylan strode toward the archway, hesitated, and then swung around to face her again. "My grandmother's right about one thing. You *do* look fetching."

And then he was gone.

Voices echoed outside the castle. Jaine propelled thoughts of sexy bosses and eccentric grandmothers from her mind. Her first visitors. Jaine's fingers white-knuckled the sides of her throne. A few seconds later, a little girl scurried in, adorable with her pigtails and sundress.

"Hello, what a beautiful day for a visit to my palace." Jaine recited a line from the manual. "I'm so happy to see you. What's your name?"

"I'm Emma!"

"Thank you for visiting, Emma. Would you like to have your picture taken with me?" Jaine slid over to make room on the wine crushed velvet cushion.

She draped her arm around Emma's back, aiming a smile as the dad snapped the picture with his camera. Emma wrapped her arms around Jaine and hugged her tight. Fuzziness warmed Jaine's insides like when she watched a Christmas movie on the Hallmark Channel.

As they separated, the little girl whispered, "Are these your real boobs?"

Jaine's fuzziness evaporated. The handbook hadn't explained how to handle that question.

And did Emma think they were genuine? Or not?

"Um. . .thank you for visiting me," Jaine stammered. "Have a wonderful day."

A redheaded boy of about five barreled into Jaine's knees harder than a defensive end sacking a quarterback on NFL Sunday. She never would have thought she'd appreciate the itchy heaps of tulle shielding her legs.

Jaine managed a dainty laugh. "What a whirlwind. Thank you for coming to see me. Would you like to join me for a picture?"

"Can I show you something first, Cinderella?" Hopeful excitement glimmered in his clear blue eyes.

"Of course."

The boy pressed his lips together, tilted his head back, and in one explosive movement rocked forward again. He blew out a jet of spit and beamed once it landed in the center of Jaine's dress. Her stomach twisting, she stared down at the glistening gob.

Dylan, I don't care how charming you are. I'm going to kill you!

"Michael, no!" his horrified mother shouted, too late.

"I can spit even further than my older cousin," Michael bragged. "I've been practicing all week. Have you ever seen anyone spit as far as me?"

Gross, gross, gross. Speechless, Jaine gaped in horror into the boy's innocent face.

"I am so sorry." His mother tugged Michael away from the throne. "I can't believe you did that!" she yelled, dragging him outside.

Jaine rubbed another section of her dress into the pool of saliva, massaging it into a damp circle. Maybe a paper towel would help. She hurtled to her feet, but inched back down when a teenage girl and boy swaggered into the castle.

Uneasiness gripping her, she registered the girl's cropped raven hair and nose ring and the boy's long concert T-shirt and ripped jeans.

"Hi Cinderella, can we ask you a few questions?" asked the girl. "We're working on a school project."

Another topic the handbooks hadn't mentioned. Was she even allowed to do interviews? And what school project involved interrogating fairy tale characters? In the summer?

"Thank you for thinking of me." Jaine spoke over the sudden mound in her throat. "What can I answer for you?"

As the boy made a couple swipes on his iPod screen and raised it to show a Record button, dread lodged in Jaine's chest. A video interview.

"We're hanging out with Cinderella at Storybook Valley today," the girl began in a smooth newscaster voice. "Cinderella, inquiring minds want to know. If you could be an animal, what kind would you be?"

Therese's orders drummed in Jaine's mind. *Don't break character. Have a creative comeback for every personal question.*

"A deer, I suppose. They're such elegant animals and we have many of them wandering throughout our forest."

"If you were a kitchen utensil, which one would you be? And why?" Her interviewer smirked.

Oh, come on. These kids were just being obnoxious.

Jaine forced a chuckle. "How amusing. Our jester must have sent you. Perhaps. . .a spoon. We have a talented chef who prepares the most delicious stew."

"A penguin walks in wearing a sombrero. What does he say and why is he here?"

Jaine tilted her head, feigning puzzlement. "A penguin? I'm afraid I don't know what that is." A family traipsed through the entrance and she concluded, "Thank you so much for this humorous interview. Have a glorious day at Storybook Valley."

And don't come back!

The afternoon passed quickly with visitors who didn't examine her chest, spit, or record stupid videos that would wind up on You Tube, though chocolate streaks stained Jaine's gown thanks to sticky ice cream hands. Storybook Valley might not attract the same crowds as the local zoo, but every family marked Cinderella's Castle on the must-see list.

Once the crowd cleared out at closing time, Jaine visited the tiny bathroom. Dabbing cold water onto her face and neck, she steadied her ragged breath. She was a business professional with a college degree.

It's temporary. Just temporary. Next year this Cinderella gig would be a distant memory. Okay, more like a nightmare, but still, she would be immersed in her marketing coordinator role, perhaps with a promotion on the horizon.

Paying her dues sucked, but she could do this.

Jaine used the toilet in her ball gown, a more challenging feat than slaying a dragon. Afterwards she backed out of the bathroom, arranging the last of her flounces. Her shift ended in fifteen minutes once all the visitors vacated the park. Jaine rotated toward her throne and froze.

Dylan clasped one hand against the wall, speaking into a walkie-talkie. He clipped it back onto his shorts and regarded her with raised brows.

A warm blush stained her cheeks. "Um, hi."

"There you are. I thought your wicked stepmother absconded with you."

The recurring flush of the toilet rang in Jaine's ears and her toes curled inside her slippers. Would the damn thing ever shut off? The cracked beige seat looked more ancient than the Cinderella tale itself, and the plumbing sounded that way too, the innards stuck and running.

"Guess we'd better get that fixed," Dylan remarked.

"Yeah. Kind of shatters the palace illusion." Maybe if she maintained a casual front, Dylan wouldn't detect her mortification.

As if the toilet comment wasn't enough, Dylan continued, "I didn't know if you'd survive a whole day without your glasses. How many fingers am I holding up?"

"Very funny. Three."

"Glad we don't have to get you a seeing-eye dog. How did it go?"

"Let's see. I got spit on, smart aleck teenagers recorded me discussing penguins in sombreros, and I discovered that children have filthy hands." Jaine didn't mention the query about breast-enhancement. That discussion would stay her and Emma's little secret. "On the bright side, I didn't wear Goth makeup, I'm not quitting, and I didn't get sick."

"I'm interested in the penguin, but I'm guessing you want to talk about something else."

"Does the phrase 'The Cinderella Curse' sound familiar?"

"Now you know why I needed someone responsible. This is probably a good time to show my appreciation, huh?" Dylan reached down and offered her a plastic bag from the floor.

Jaine lifted out an aqua hooded sweatshirt with Storybook Valley spelled out in white letters. He remembered. She hadn't expected him to follow through, at least not so soon. "My sweatshirt! Thank you!" She examined the inside tag. Medium. "You even got the right size. I'm impressed."

"I asked Krystal's advice," Dylan admitted. "I put gold stars in the bag, too. You can trade them for prizes at our Rides Party on Friday night."

Okay, maybe she wouldn't kill him.

"Well, thanks. I have to agree that Cinderella has put you through the wringer between the vomiting in the castle, purple hair, and tattoos."

"This park needs a publicist. How about we meet after work tomorrow? We can figure out the best marketing project for you to tackle this summer."

"Sounds great. Is it all right if I share some ideas?"

"Sure. I'll walk you to Wardrobe and we can start discussing it." Dylan's walkie-talkie beeped. He unclipped it from his side and pressed a button. "Yeah?"

A burst of static crackled and a male voice responded, "There's a situation at the basketball toss. A dad is freaking out because he wants a bigger stuffed animal for his kid and he won't leave. Can you help?"

"I'll be right there." Dylan sighed and replaced the walkie-talkie. "Sorry. I'd better handle this."

Disappointment sliced through Jaine, surprising her with its strength. "That's okay, another time. Thanks again for the sweatshirt. I love that color. Did Krystal help you pick it out?"

"Actually, it reminded me of your eyes. Blue like the ocean."

He had noticed her eyes. Dylan's serious green ones bore into hers, tripping her pulse. The air between them seemed electrified.

He combed a lock of hair off his face. "I'd better go," he said quietly.

Left alone, Jaine fingered the fleecy lining of the sweatshirt. After a few seconds, she awakened from her daze. No. She would not fall for her boss.

That would be even more disastrous than spitballs on the princess dress.

Chapter Five

You Are Cordially Invited to Our Back-to-School Ball. Join us for a special menu, school songs, and dancing. Collect autographs and fun facts from your favorite characters.

Jaine stopped typing and reread the words on the screen. She rolled her shoulders, loosening her stiff neck. She'd labored over the computer tucked in the corner of her stuffy living room for an hour and a half. A tabletop fan whirred from a folding chair, but neither the blowing air nor her thin nightgown decreased her sweating.

Willow purred from her desk, leaning forward to sniff Jaine's damp shampooed hair. Soon the sniff progressed into a series of licks.

"You rascal." Jaine scooped up the ebony cat and dumped her on the cream carpet. Willow bolted down the hallway and into the dim kitchen, challenging Jaine to a chase.

"Sorry, cutie, I'm busy."

If Jaine wanted to pitch this proposal to Dylan, lots more work stretched ahead. She needed to brainstorm details, design a sample flyer, and create a low-budget marketing plan that would encourage media buzz and higher attendance.

Boy that sounded daunting. Her fingers froze on the keyboard.

Okay, she had convinced kids she was freaking Cinderella.

That proved she could succeed at anything. Jaine squared her shoulders and resumed typing.

***

The next evening, Dylan leafed through the packet Jaine had three-hole punched into a presentation folder. Restless, she rubbed a palm over her pants leg. She'd changed out of her costume and into a casual business suit.

Jaine skimmed her own set of papers, identical to Dylan's, waiting for him to finish. She adjusted her glasses, grateful for their familiar comfort. Her fingers twisted into knots.

Despite her uneasiness, Jaine knew she had outlined solid ideas. She had pitched the Back-to-School Ball and a Halloween costume ball, fun family activities to attract locals.

Dylan closed the folder and placed it on his overflowing desk. Jaine wondered if he would ever find it again.

"I appreciate your enthusiasm, but with our budget constraints, I was thinking of something simpler, like another ad campaign for the water park."

Was he kidding? She'd asked if it was okay to share her ideas and he'd replied yes.

"Summer is half over and people have their vacations planned," Jaine said. "We want to promote the water park hook for *next* summer. To maximize ticket sales in the meantime, you've got to target locals who might make an impulse day trip and give them a reason to plan a visit into their hectic schedules."

"Your proposal is creative, but now isn't the right time. This would require a lot of overtime, and I can't pay that. Anyway, I'd need to know estimated expenses and projected revenue."

Jaine compressed her lips. "It wouldn't take many extra hours. My hospital supervisor always commented on my efficiency. Regarding expenses, most newspapers and regional parenting magazines have community calendars. We can promote these activities at no charge. You can't promote the water park for free because there's no event tied to it."

A crease cut between his brows as if he feared her transforming into the Evil Queen from *Snow White*. "I still need hard numbers."

"Then let's crunch some. I spent all this time putting the proposal together. You could at least explore it before saying no."

He responded with a stony look and silence.

Uh oh. The twins called Jaine defensive. Her parents dubbed her oversensitive. Whatever the right adjective was, it meant that Jaine wasn't the most diplomatic person in the world and sometimes she didn't recognize her shadow side emerging until it was too late.

"Anyone ever tell you that you're stubborn?" Dylan asked.

"I may have heard that once or twice. Among other things."

Bree had used the term "pain in the butt," but she didn't share that tidbit.

"You win. Let's discuss it, but this conversation is in theory. I can't promise anything without a cost analysis. Deal?"

She dipped her head in a reluctant nod. "The Back-to-School Ball is an excuse to get us mentioned in the media. They're always hunting for fresh back-to-school angles so it's a good opportunity for coverage."

Jaine scuffed her chair a few inches closer to the desk. "For

Halloween, kids would trick or treat through the park. Then everyone gathers for dinner and dancing to Halloween music. You decorate anyway, so this just adds another element."

"What about food? Entertainment?"

Jaine consulted the spiral-bound notebook she had slid into the pocket of her own folder. "I thought burgers, hotdogs, fries, and salad with cookies or ice cream for dessert. At the school event, Jack and Jill from the afternoon kids' show could sing songs like the *ABC Song*, *The Wheels on the Bus*, and *Mary Had a Little Lamb*. We'd set up the stage into a classroom with a chalkboard and desks. At the end, we'd hand out diplomas showing that the kids graduated from Storybook Valley School. None of those things would mean spinning straw into gold."

Oops, she might have crossed the sarcasm line with that last comment.

"The main expenses come from paying staff members," she added.

He opened his folder and turned a few pages. "What's this autograph book filled with facts?"

"We'd use the books from the gift shop and every character writes an educational fact alongside their name. Like 'Remember Your Vowels, A-E-I-O-and-U, Love Mother Goose.'"

Damn, it was hard to sound professional when referencing Mother Goose.

"If we went forward—and that's a big *if*—"

"Yeah, yeah, trust me, I got that." Jaine rolled her eyes.

"You're sure working on this wouldn't be too stressful? On top of your other hours, it would cut into your downtime."

"I don't mind. The Meet and Greets wind down soon so

58

things will get less hectic. How about August twenty-ninth?"

"It would have to be the weekend before that. Our annual Employee Appreciation Cookout is the last Saturday in August, and after that, most of our staff goes back to school."

The earlier weekend would conflict with Bree's wedding. Crap.

"My sister is getting married then. I meant to ask about leaving early Friday and Saturday for the rehearsal and wedding. If we scheduled the balls for that weekend—and yes, I know it's a big *if*, but assuming the Three Little Pigs sprout wings and you pursue the idea—I wouldn't be there to oversee the last-minute details and you'd need to use your backup Cinderella."

Jaine winced during a long pause. Dylan would hate fooling around with the Cinderella schedule again. "I know, here I am talking about how organized and responsible I am, and I forgot to tell you that I need time off."

"I'm just wrapping my head around the image of the Three Little Pigs sprouting wings. As far as the park being down a Cinderella, I'll see if I can schedule Wendy to cover your shifts. Any other life-altering events on your calendar? Christenings? Bar Mitzvahs?"

"That's it, or else I'd be so crazed you'd have to lock me in a tower." Jaine scanned her copy of the back-to-school flyer.

This was her brainchild. If plans proceeded, she'd have to miss it. Not that there was a chance in hell of the ball going forward since this discussion was just to appease her, and even if by some miracle Dylan was considering it, her schedule conflict gave him the perfect excuse to decline.

"Honestly, I'd much rather be here, than stuck at a wedding

ceremony looking like a piece of bubblegum," she muttered.

"Bubblegum?"

"My sister Bree picked Tutti Frutti bridesmaid dresses. Since you're a guy, I'm sure you don't understand what this means. The bridesmaids will look like a pack of Hubba Bubba on the dance floor."

Dylan grinned. "That pushed the flying pigs out of my head. Be sure to bring in pictures."

"Yeah, right. I'll do that when the Three Little Pigs fly."

"All this talking is making me thirsty. Want some lemonade?"

"I'd love one." Jaine rose along with Dylan. "Is there any in the fridge?"

"Not bottled lemonade. The real kind. You know, from a lemon?"

"You mean like they sell in the park? Aren't the stands closed?"

"I think we can get around that. I heard the owners are pretty cool."

Jaine followed him outside into the ninety-degree humidity. Heat flared up from the sunbaked asphalt. They walked down the path and passed a perspiring girl shuffling a broom along a trail of scattered caramel corn.

Dylan paused beside a rotund maintenance man pushing a cart loaded with garbage bags. "Hey, Harold."

"Dylan!" Gray streaked his rumpled hair, bushy eyebrows, and thick walrus mustache. He tapped the pedometer attached to his shorts pocket. "Two miles so far today. Not bad for an old guy, huh?"

"You're in better shape than all of us. I'd like you to meet Jaine, our new marketing coordinator. She's also helping out as Cindy for a few months. Jaine, this is Harold, our head of maintenance."

Harold pumped Jaine's hand. "Pleased to meet you. I've known this kid since he was five. Have you ever heard what a hell raiser he was?"

"A hell raiser? Dylan? Tell me more." Jaine leaned forward.

"Let's see. . .once when he was about nine, Dylan and his brother took the train out for a joy ride. Boy, did they get in hot water with their parents. Then there was the time he snuck in with his friends and had a midnight keg party on the Swan Princess."

Dylan groaned and kicked a pebble off the path with his sneaker. "Thanks for the boost to my professional image, Harold. Appreciate it."

"You always livened up the place, fella. We missed you around here. I miss that brother of yours, too. Any chance Jake will come back?"

"I don't think so. It's complicated. Rory will be here for Rides Night though. You coming?"

"Wouldn't miss it. Oh!" Harold's ruddy face brightened. He fumbled into his shorts pocket and withdrew a silver child-sized locket and a worn stuffed duck rattle. "I stumbled across these while I was sweeping. I'll put them in Lost and Found."

"Great, thanks. Harold is a master at reuniting people with lost objects," Dylan explained to Jaine. "He likes to follow up with Guest Relations to see which items were claimed."

"I sure hate to think of kids missing their blankets and toys. I'd better get back to work. Nice meeting you, Jaine. See you at Rides Night, Dylan." Harold gave a deep rumbling laugh.

"Don't get into any trouble."

Jaine and Dylan continued down the pathway past the carousel.

"A keg party on the boat? Really?" she asked with a speculative glance.

"I got grounded for the whole summer. My aunt and uncle run the Storybook Valley Inn and Grill down the street. They saw lights in the park and called my dad." Dylan shot her a crooked smile that made Jaine's heart beat faster. "Seemed like a good idea at seventeen."

"Your brother wasn't involved?"

"That wasn't his scene. My sister Rory wasn't part of it, either. They tried talking me out of it, but didn't turn me in. They enjoyed it when I got caught though."

Dylan stopped at a hut with a thatched roof and a view of the dormant Ferris wheel. Jaine waited at the counter while he entered the back door. Within a minute, he was slicing a lemon on a cutting board, spearing straight down the middle into two circles.

"You've done this before," Jaine observed.

"Only a thousand times. This was one of my summer jobs in high school. My parents expected us to work at the park." Dylan fitted a lemon onto a squeezer and pressed down, dribbling juice into a bowl. "How about you? Did you have a summer job?"

"Grocery store cashier. Didn't like it much. Long lines, grouchy customers. I preferred my volunteer job, teaching computer skills to senior citizens."

"How did you get into teaching?" Dylan combined juice, sugar, and water in a pitcher and stirred with a tall spoon.

"It started as a National Honor Society project, but I liked

62

it so much that I volunteered for a couple years until. . . things got busy at home." Jaine omitted her mother's illness, the reason for the chaos.

"That was nice of you." Dylan paused, his hand on the wooden spoon. "I didn't see that on your resume."

"I never thought to include it. It didn't seem like a big deal."

"I'll bet it was a big deal to the people you helped." He poured the contents into two cups of ice and garnished the drinks with lemons. Dylan affixed plastic covers, inserted straws through the lids, and slid her cup across the counter. "Here you go, ma'am."

Jaine sipped the sugary liquid while Dylan washed a few dishes. "This is delicious! Thank you."

A few minutes later, he emerged from the hut and beckoned her to follow again. "Let's go somewhere shady."

Soon, he and Jaine sat side-by-side on a shaded bench facing the pond. During the day, the creamy white Swan Princess ferried passengers every fifteen minutes, but tonight it remained docked at the wooden pier. Sunlight dappled the shimmering pond, framed by a canvas of mountain greenery. Jagged peaks rose above the white sheet of clouds.

A squirrel scampered across the grass, carrying an acorn.

"How cute!" Jaine loved anything furry.

"Cute," Dylan scoffed. "Those critters have chewed off electrical wiring under the antique cars and eaten through Red Riding Hood's log cabin. My dad uses a homemade spray of jalapeno pepper, cayenne pepper, and tabasco sauce to keep them away."

"It actually works?"

"I wouldn't have believed it, either, but it does. That and

the feeding station my family set up. My mother created a squirrel oasis where she leaves out peanut butter and sunflower seeds. Apparently, we have an agreement with those rodents."

"I guess nature has its drawbacks." Jaine breathed in the fresh air. "Still, I love the Catskills. I can't imagine living anywhere else."

"Me either. I'm always doing something outdoors. Skiing, snowboarding, mountain biking, canoeing, hiking. What are you into?"

"I'm content sitting outside reading a book. I suppose hiking's okay if the trail isn't too steep."

"Ever ski?"

"No." Jaine trembled with a mock shiver. "I'd be too cold."

"Not if you dress warm. There's nothing like night skiing, riding under the lights, moon, and stars. Then you can relax and read by a crackling fire." He nudged her arm. "I'll have to give you lessons."

Mmm, that sounded cozy, especially with Dylan teaching.

"That's right. You mentioned that you were a ski instructor. How did you wind up back at Storybook Valley?" Jaine studied him, brimming with curiosity.

She couldn't envision him in such a different work environment. Even though she had only known him for a couple days, it seemed as if Dylan belonged at the helm of the theme park.

Dylan didn't answer right away and Jaine sensed he was choosing his words with care. "I grew up watching my parents plan employee cookouts and hand out gold stars. I thought every company was like that. Pretty naïve. Eventually I realized how fortunate we were to own a successful business. After my dad's heart attack, I talked to my family about taking over."

"What would've happened if you didn't step forward?"

"They would have hired a manager from within, or taken one of the offers they've gotten to sell the park."

"It must have relieved your parents when you saved the day." Then Jaine noticed the tense set to Dylan's shoulders.

She recalled Therese's disapproval of the new marketing position and her insistence they obey the park's procedures "regardless of what Dylan told you." He was working so hard to learn the business and reinvigorate Storybook Valley. Even she, a newcomer, saw it. Jaine hoped his family recognized it, too.

Dylan uncapped his drink and poked the straw around, hunting for the last droplets of lemonade between ice chunks. He deposited it on the grass, giving up. "Not exactly. They groomed my older brother Jake to run the park. He was the responsible one, and I wasn't. My sister wanted to focus on dancing so they taught Jake the ins and outs of the business. He even got an MBA."

"Why didn't he take over?"

"He met a girl at one of my parties. They dated for a month or two and she got pregnant." Dylan sighed and passed a hand through his blond hair. "This girl was a total flake. She moved back to Maine to be near her mom and stepfather, who are even more unreliable than she is. Jake lived with her for a while, but they finally broke up and he found a place a couple blocks away. He hasn't been able to get full custody, so he's stuck there."

"He made a mistake but accepted the consequences. That's admirable."

"Rory and I think so, but my parents insist he screwed up his life. They're so damn stubborn that they never see him or their granddaughter. They weren't thrilled I took over instead of Jake. Guess I can't blame them. I've been swearing since high school I wanted nothing to do with this place." Dylan stared into the rippling pond, his face steely.

A surge of anger welled up inside Jaine. Didn't the Callahans understand that their sons had grown up? Instead of obsessing about Cinderella's signature, maybe they should consider their children's feelings. Dylan's family lived in a soap opera rather than a fairy tale.

Jaine laid a light hand on his tanned bicep. "All teens rebel against their parents and make stupid decisions. That was a long time ago. You saved them heartache by taking over and it looks like you're doing a great job. I'm sure they'll come to appreciate that."

Dylan's eyes fastened on her. Self-conscious, Jaine retracted her hand and buckled it around her drained cup.

"I can't believe I told you all this," Dylan said, his expression perplexed. "It must have been bugging me more than I thought. Thanks for listening, Jaine."

His words infused her with enough courage to continue in counselor mode. She set the cup beside her on the bench.

"Stop feeling guilty for things you did as a kid. Every teenager mouths off to his parents. My mom used to tell my sisters and me that what goes around, comes around, and to wait till we're parents."

"Your mom sounds like a smart lady."

"She was. She died when I was in college. Cancer." Jaine's throat thickened. It always did when people asked about her mother.

A frown ridged Dylan's forehead. "I'm sorry. That must have been terrible. I noticed on your resume that you took awhile to earn your bachelor's degree. Was that why?"

"I dropped out to be with her. At first, my mother wanted me to march right back to school and tell them I made a mistake. But I could finish college anytime, and once she started chemo and radiation, my mom was glad I'd stayed. Her treatment was aggressive and there were a lot of appointments."

"What about your sisters? Didn't they help out?"

"They did their best, but one had a baby and the other was studying for law school. I was a freshman, so I'd barely started school anyway."

"What you did, that was remarkable, Jaine. Not everyone would be so unselfish, especially a college kid." Dylan reached over and squeezed her hand.

Jaine observed their interlaced fingers, a funny tingling rising up inside her.

"I think you're pretty remarkable, too." She raised her head to find Dylan watching her, mere inches away. She hadn't noticed the stubble on his chin and resisted the urge to run her thumb along the rough patch.

Suddenly, Dylan leaned forward and covered her mouth with his. Heart thundering, Jaine nestled closer and deepened the kiss. A jolt of heat zoomed through her. *This is really happening. I'm kissing Dylan Callahan.*

It felt surreal. Amazing. Insane.

She was kissing Dylan Callahan. Her boss.

Oh my God!

They disengaged, breathing hard. Uneasiness quaked through Jaine and a flush climbed her throat. What had she done? She wanted Dylan and his family to respect her and here she was making out with her boss after two days on the job.

Dylan slid further down the bench and rubbed the middle of his forehead. "That was my fault. I shouldn't have. . .I can't believe I. . . ."

"It wasn't just you." Jaine avoided eye contact. "I've never done anything like that. Not with my boss. Of course, my last couple supervisors were women, and the one before that was sixty, but, I know how inappropriate this was and—"

Dylan's grim voice cut over her babbling. "I have done this kind of thing. . .with customers when I was a teenager. I challenged myself to see how many girls' phone numbers I could collect. Hiring an attractive woman and romancing her is just what my family would expect."

A giggle escaped Jaine and then another one. She wasn't just a harlot; she was a hysterical harlot. Dylan gaped at her as if her clothes had transformed into tatters.

"No offense, but did that really work? You'd serve girls lemonade, and they'd just hand over their phone numbers and let you 'romance' them?"

"I got more numbers when I was a ride operator at the rollercoaster," Dylan answered slowly, "but yeah, basically they succumbed to my charm."

That triggered another round of chuckles. Jaine couldn't stop even though her thoughts threatened to sober her. "Maybe they were desperate if they let themselves get picked up at a children's theme park."

Despite his earlier graveness, a smile unfurled on Dylan's lips. "You just kissed me, didn't you?"

"I kissed you *back*!" Jaine slouched forward and buried her face in her hands. "Sorry, I laugh when I'm nervous. Can we forget this whole thing ever happened?"

She braved a look at her boss. Dylan's smile slipped away. "I'm glad we're on the same wavelength. I was afraid you might file a sexual harassment claim. Honestly, I didn't mean to put you in an uncomfortable position. I promise, Jaine, it won't happen again."

Jaine didn't dare admit that the position had been quite comfortable, thank you very much. "You weren't harassing me. I'm worried you'll think less of me and I'll have to search for another job. I was so relieved to work for a company that devotes itself to families having fun, not something boring like, I don't know, selling shampoo, or sporting goods."

She was rambling again.

"I promise, you won't be cast out onto the street to sell shampoo," Dylan said. "I guess I just find you easy to talk to and got carried away. We both had baggage on our minds and—"

"Right. Baggage makes people vulnerable." Jaine nodded vigorously.

"But we both agree that given our employer/employee status, it's best to keep our relationship professional, so that's what we'll do. Problem solved."

"We won't ever speak of this again." She retrieved both cups and jumped to her feet. Time to escape and wallow in a pint of chocolate chip ice cream. "I should go."

Dylan stood. "We can still be friends, though, right?"

"Of course. All workplaces should have a friendly environment. It's good for morale."

"And for the record, I do take you seriously, Jaine. I think we make a good team. Marketing team, I mean."

They lingered in silence until Dylan wished her a good

night just as Jaine thanked him for the lemonade. She lifted one cup in an awkward wave and strode back to the winding path. Jaine discarded the cups into a trash receptacle and made the long walk toward the employee exit.

Harold hunched behind the Guest Relations' Desk sifting through the overflowing Lost and Found pile. The duck rattle, locket, a sweatshirt, wallet, and an unopened bag of Doritos Cool Ranch Flavored Tortilla Chips lined the counter, awaiting their turn into the deep plastic bin.

"Hi there, Jaine, did you and Dylan have a nice break?" Harold aimed a grin at her.

Was it her imagination or was it a knowing grin? A grin that implied, "You were just in a lip lock with your boss."

Jaine tugged a strand of hair behind her ear, praying Harold hadn't seen anything. "It was fine. We've been brainstorming about a marketing idea involving. . .Cinderella and Prince Charming. We were acting out an upcoming photo shoot."

"Photo shoot?" Sounding doubtful, Harold tossed the Doritos bag into the Lost and Found.

Jaine wondered if tomorrow one of the Guest Services staff members would crunch into the tortilla chips on her lunch break. "Right. See you later!"

She increased her strides toward the employee exit gate. Maybe she would have a glass of wine—or three—with her ice cream.

Chapter Six

"What do you mean, you're not coming to my bachelorette party?" With each word, Bree's voice rose one decibel. "I need both my sisters there. How can you skip my party? You've had plenty of notice."

Yes, because I organized it.

Jaine inched her cell phone away from her ear as her Bridezilla sister launched into a guilt trip. She pressed against the balcony, peering over the railing. Down below, her neighbor barbecued for his girlfriend on the grass between Jaine's building and the next one in the complex. Smoke wafted from the grill, flavoring the air with the charred scents of burgers.

She imagined an intimate dinner with Dylan, and a deep pang shuddered inside Jaine. *No, don't go there.*

She hadn't dated anyone more than a few times since her college boyfriend Logan dumped her after her mother's diagnosis. Once she was no longer available to help him study or write his papers, Logan's interest waned. She'd had occasional dates, but no one exciting.

Back in February, Jaine went out with the cousin of her married college friend. They'd had an okay dinner, but no sparks kindled during the good night kiss and Jaine made up an excuse the next time he called. As every Northeast girl understood, (except for her friend, who stopped setting up Jaine on blind dates) winter was too damn cold to venture out at night when there were no sparks.

Jaine would brave a blizzard for another kiss with Dylan Callahan. Loneliness sweeping over her, she pictured the long lonely evening ahead. It figured. The one guy who interested her was off-limits.

She hunkered onto her patio chair as Bree ran out of words. "I'm not skipping your bachelorette party. Just missing dinner. I'll still come to the club."

"Dinner's the most important part," Bree snapped. "Later, we'll be so drunk we won't know if you're there or not. Are you even riding in the limo?"

"I'll take my car and meet you." Jaine could have predicted aggravation from Bree, but she hadn't expected such passion. Could her sister care that much about her presence?

"You're a bridesmaid. You're supposed to attend bridesmaid events!"

"Excuse me, but who got migraines planning your bridal shower for June, because you were petrified your guests would be on vacation if we waited too long?" Shauna, the maid of honor, should have organized the shower, but since Jaine had a simpler schedule, she got elected instead.

"It *was* a nice shower," Bree admitted.

"Glad you liked it. Sorry about the bachelorette party, but I have to work. If you get appetizers and hang out for a while, I may make it for dessert."

Dylan had granted her time off for the rehearsal and wedding, but no way was Jaine blowing off a Meet and Greet to drink with her sister's friends. Besides, despite Bree's hurt, anger, sense of betrayal, or whatever, she would ignore Jaine at the restaurant, distracted by her friends and her twin.

"What marketing happens at seven o'clock at night?" Bree asked.

Jaine began the cover story she had concocted. "We're producing a new brochure and hired a photographer to come that night. I have to stick with him."

This mythical photographer was busy between the Cinderella project she'd invented for Harold and now attending the Meet and Greet.

"Can't someone else do that?" Bree asked.

"I'm the marketing coordinator. Redoing the brochure was my idea. I've got to make sure it comes out right."

"It had to be that night?"

Jaine balled the napkin leftover from her ice cream and wine snack. "Would you prefer it to be during the wedding or rehearsal? The photographer was booked solid and there wasn't much choice. Besides, I can't ask for all that time off. I'm brand new."

"But—"

"Sabreena! I have to work. End of story. I'll get there when I can unless you continue to irritate me. Then I'll stay home and read in the bathtub."

What an Un-Cinderella thing to say. That made it more rewarding.

"I. . .I. . . ."

Yeah, yeah. Jaine waited for indignation to crackle through the line. Her neighbor down below delved into a grocery bag, exposing a package of marshmallows and two skewers. His girlfriend kissed him firm on the lips.

Some girls were princesses and others just pretended.

"Sorry I'm a bitchy bride," Bree said. "When I was growing up, imagining my wedding day, I never dreamed I'd get married without Mom. It helps to have you and Shauna. It's like part of her is still with me."

Bree's voice sounded tight, choked. Perhaps she was suffering an anaphylactic reaction to the word 'Sorry.' Jaine expected her sister to rattle off countless more problems in the coming weeks, but for now she accepted the olive branch.

"I know. I miss her, too."

Jaine didn't add that their mother would have loved attending bridal fittings. Coordinating the shower. Offering input on cake, flowers, and color schemes. Gently convincing her daughter to choose Venetian Gold bridesmaid gowns. Jaine hadn't considered how heart wrenching it must be for Bree to plan a wedding without their mother. Even with Mom's presence, her sister would have acted bitchy, because, well, Bree was Bree. . .but their mother always reprimanded her.

"I miss Dad, too." Bree huffed out a sob. "Whenever I call, Gloria answers. She acts so phony, asking about the wedding and then hinting how much trouble it is for them to come. Their neighbor has to walk the dog, they're missing a condo association meeting, her daughter needs to hire a babysitter. . .what does she want me to do, offer her the Stepmother of the Year Award?"

"At least she asks how you're doing. All she discusses with me are her grandchildren."

Gloria wasn't a wicked stepmother—exactly—but she didn't appreciate the sacrifice Jaine's father made by moving to Florida. What a sacrifice they all made.

"Sorry, Jaine, I'm just exhausted. I understand why you can't get there early and that your job is important. I don't mean to take you for granted."

Where was a recording device when you needed one?

Then Jaine could replay the words next time she felt like strangling Breezilla.

"It's okay. Planning a wedding is hard work."

After they hung up, Jaine spent a couple hours at her computer fulfilling a promise to her other overwhelmed sister, researching after-school programs. One expensive day care center offered drama, swimming, crafts, and character development, while another smaller program seemed geared toward free play and homework aid. An in-between sized site included private piano or voice lessons. Then there were several home-based centers where kids could run around in a backyard and use the swing set.

By 11 p.m., Jaine's shoulders ached and her bleary eyes struggled to stay open. No, she refused to let sleep triumph. She needed to cross this task off her to-do list. Jaine created a Word file listing the price, web site, and benefits of each program, emailed it to Shauna, and exhaled.

Wrung out, Jaine shut down her computer and went to bed.

***

Friday night at dusk, Jaine and a dozen fairy tale characters awaited the train for the Meet and Greet. They stood behind the fence separating the employee bungalows from the rest of the theme park. She didn't envy the college kids stuck inside the heavy Dazzle the Dragon and Gingerbread Man costumes. They wore T-shirts and shorts in the dressing room until the time arrived to don suits and headpieces.

Jaine couldn't imagine how they could see, let alone breathe, beneath those humongous heads. Both characters stood silent, conserving energy. Soon the Gingerbread Man would scurry around in his brown felt jumpsuit etched with frosting and peppermints, pretending to flee from hungry children. Dazzle would bounce and dance in the plush green mascot costume, orange-trimmed tail flopping.

Jaine fingered her elegant ball gown. Things could be worse.

"Hi, Your Highness, I'm home." A young man in his mid-to-late twenties joined her on the grass, closing the door to the wardrobe cottage behind him.

Jaine gawked at his white military style jacket with attached epaulets and royal blue slacks. A jeweled crown capped his black hair and a gold jacquard sash crossed his torso. Ah. Prince Charming. He fit the role with his dark good looks, six foot height, and straight posture. If he lost the prince duds, Jaine could visualize him in a car commercial.

"You know. . .because we're supposed to be married?" he prodded. "Instead of 'Hi, honey, I'm home,' it's— "

"Your Highness. Right. I'm Jaine."

"Sean. Though I respond to Your Majesty. Your Royal Highness. Your Greatness. Take your pick."

"I'll stick with Sean." Jaine laughed. "How long have you been part of the Royal Family?"

"The last few years. When I'm not making children smile, I'm performing at a local dinner theater or going on auditions. I did a gig on a soap opera. Maybe you saw it. Simon on *Tomorrow's Destiny*?" He sounded hopeful.

This guy *could* star in a commercial. "I don't watch that show, but congratulations. How exciting." She motioned to her translucent shoes. "When I'm not wearing glass slippers, I'm the park's new marketing coordinator."

"Cool."

Therese walked by them and paused, though Jaine almost didn't recognize her with the granny glasses roosted on the bridge of her nose, floral print flannel nightgown, and matching nightcap topping her wig of springy white coils. Beside Therese, a man in his early sixties inspected Jaine from tiara to glass slippers. Despite his shaggy brows, mustache and beard, she recognized a trace of Dylan in his features. Everything else reminded her of Santa Claus scrutinizing a culprit from the Naughty List.

Jaine couldn't pinpoint whom Mr. Callahan was portraying in his work shirt, apron with tools extending out the front pocket, and pointed leather shoes. Not Santa, despite the resemblance. She couldn't guess Therese's character, either, until she glimpsed Krystal/Red Riding Hood a few feet away.

Jaine snapped her fingers. "You're Red Riding Hood's grandmother."

Therese nodded. "And this is my husband, Will. He's the shoemaker from *The Elves and the Shoemaker*."

"How fun that the shoemaker takes part in the Meet and Greets," Jaine said. "I love that diorama scene in the park and the kids enjoyed the story when I read it the other day."

Mr. Callahan examined her long and hard. Jaine shifted her weight, uncomfortable in her "glass" slippers. Feigning interest in cobbler elves wasn't enough to win over the king of Storybook Valley.

"This is Jaine Andersen," Therese informed her husband. "Dylan's marketing coordinator."

"We've never had a marketing coordinator." Mr. Callahan grimaced, still eyeing Jaine.

"I can't believe how many details you've managed over the years. Not only maintaining the rides, but expanding them, and overseeing the shows, food, staff, and advertising. It's amazing." Although Jaine hoped to flatter, she spoke the truth. The Callahans' accomplishments impressed her. . .but what worked five decades ago wouldn't help the park flourish today.

"It's hardly amazing. We got along just fine."

Lois Callahan saved her from more awkward conversation with Mr. Callahan. Lois floated over in a full-length rose organdy and brocade ball gown with an embroidered bodice and layered tiered skirts. Lois clasped a glittery silver wand that matched the large wings attached to the back of her gown. "Hello, my dear. Tonight you will address me as Fairy Godmother. Upon meeting a child, you shall ask, 'Have you visited with Fairy Godmother yet?' That will enhance the authenticity."

Oh, my.

"I'll do that," Jaine said.

"I see you have met our accomplished young thespian, Sean." Lois beamed at Prince Charming before sweeping a critical glance over Jaine.

Uh oh. For the first time, Jaine had managed her own makeup without Krystal's aid. The lash curler freaked her out, but she mastered it and was mighty proud of herself.

"Jaine does not understand stage presence so we must prepare her." Lois drilled out orders and Jaine did her best to obey. "Head high. Shoulders back. Stomach tight."

Lois jabbed the wand in the air to punctuate each statement. "Keep your center. Now smile. No, no, that won't do. That looks too plastic."

"Have you ever seen an Audrey Hepburn movie, Jaine?" Sean asked. "That might help. She had a regal screen presence."

"Marvelous idea." Lois's face brightened. "Yes, you must watch *Roman Holiday*."

"And *My Fair Lady*," Sean put in.

"Excellent suggestion. Both films will give brilliant examples for you to follow, Jaine."

Jaine spotted the Fairy Tale Express chugging down the track and prayed it would arrive before they assigned more old films. The train slowed to a grating halt on the track outside the fence.

"All aboard!" called the engineer, an elderly man in a checkered cap, shirt, and overalls. He sat sideways on a tan cushion and blew Lois a kiss.

Her cheeks pinkening, Lois joined him up front. All the characters greeted him before choosing a seat. Even Dazzle and the Gingerbread Man waved chubby velour hands.

Jaine boarded the blue-and-white canopied locomotive and scooted over to make room for Sean on the wooden bench. "Is that Lois's husband?"

"Yeah, wait till you meet him. He and Lois are total opposite since she's so formal and he's fun-loving."

It sounded as if Dylan took after his grandfather. With a piercing whistle, the train rumbled down the track, and they traveled past the bakery, antique cars, and a gift shop. The park would close to the public after the fireworks though employees could remain for the staff Rides Night. Jaine wasn't sure what to expect, but she planned to stick with Krystal.

The Fairy Tale Express stopped at Castle Cookery, the biggest eating area in the park. Pink and yellow turrets rose from a domed roof and dozens of round tables, plastic chairs, and stone benches scattered the cement floor. Jaine and

Amber had lunched here, loading their trays inside the nearby cafeteria and toting the food out to a table. Now guests waited outside, assembled for the Meet and Greet.

"Time to get out those autograph books and cameras!" Dylan's grandfather announced over a microphone. "Our characters will be available in the courtyard for the next thirty minutes. They'll lead the children in a parade and usher in our magnificent fireworks display!"

Sean disembarked from the train and offered his hand. "Your Highness?"

Man, he got into the whole royal thing. Jaine stepped to the pavement. Cameras and phones captured the intimacy of Prince Charming and Cinderella.

The Fairy Tale Paparazzi.

"Cinderella! Can I get your autograph?" A little girl scooted up to Jaine, thrusting a red crayon and a coloring book into her face.

Jaine wrote in her best Cinderella signature, but by the time the Meet and Greet session ended, her penmanship deteriorated to doctor-illegible. Luckily Lois relished her fairy godmother part too much to inspect Jaine's writing. The characters and a line of children paraded around Castle Cookery, marching to lively music until the first light bursts spangled overhead. Jaine held the small hands of two little girls as they admired the display together.

Glowing embers tumbled in the air, flickering back and forth while they fell to earth. A flower with points of light streaking outward graced the sky followed by a series of flaming balls. Explosions boomed one after another. Mesmerized kids watched delicate trails of gold that shimmered for a full ten seconds.

The familiar but long forgotten scent of smoke floated in the light breeze. Jaine hadn't seen fireworks since the celebrations of her adolescence. She'd considered attending her town's July Fourth display, but most of her friends had moved or were busy with significant others and she hadn't wanted to show up alone.

Here, everyone coveted time with her. Okay, most were age four, but still. Weekend fireworks displays were a definite job perk.

After the grand finale, Jaine and the other characters waved at the families streaming toward the exit. She even remembered elbow, elbow, wrist, wrist though she hadn't mastered the technique.

Once the guests left the park, the characters changed out of their costumes in the wardrobe cottage. A headless Dazzle the Dragon waited for Krystal to help him out of the puffy suit, his hair a mass of plastered sweat.

Storybook Valley, behind the scenes. When she was a kid, Jaine never wondered where Dazzle, Cinderella, Little Red Riding Hood, and the rest of the cast hung out off-duty or considered that they were real people wearing costumes. To Jaine, they'd been Dazzle, Cinderella, and Little Red Riding Hood. Now children viewed *her* as Cinderella. Strange.

A half hour later, hundreds of employees gathered at the picnic pavilion near the back of the park. They clustered at pastel purple and blue tables and milled in small groups on the lawn. In the distance, the blazing spokes of the Ferris wheel revolved in the darkness and colored waterslide tubes twisted high in the air.

Jaine glimpsed Dylan and his father each manning a huge gas grill while Lois and Therese monitored supplies of chips,

81

coleslaw, and water bottles. Jaine hadn't seen Dylan since The Mistake.

Her pulse skittering, she whipped her head back toward Krystal. They were inspecting a long table strewn with Storybook Valley hats, T-shirts, and fanny packs, along with vouchers for free meals at the concession stands, movie passes, and gift cards to local shops and restaurants. "How do the gold stars work?"

Krystal had shed her Red Riding Hood outfit for a beaded top, black leggings, and heels, making Jaine feel underdressed in her Storybook Valley sweatshirt and jeans. "You can either turn in stars tonight for a smaller prize or save up for a gift card. There's an opportunity to redeem them at every employee event."

As Jaine debated whether to select a T-shirt or hold out for a certificate to a local craft store, Krystal introduced her to the wispy blonde behind the table. "This is Tiara, Dylan's cousin and my oldest friend in the world. Her family owns the Storybook Valley Inn and Grill down the road. This is Jaine, the new marketing coordinator and temporary Cindy."

Jaine never heard of anyone named after a crown before, but it suited this young woman with her golden coils sparkling with sequin flower combs. Tiara's whole face sparkled. Her eyes shone with gold shadow on the lids and pink glitter underneath them. Tiny rhinestones twinkled along her lash line, a style Jaine had never seen except in *Vogue*. Even her blush twinkled.

"What a beautiful name," Jaine said. "I always wanted a more exciting name than Jaine."

Tiara laughed, straightening a row of restaurant gift cards. "My family thrives on exciting names. Mom's Gretel and my siblings are Cas, from *Prince Caspian: The Return to Narnia*, and Wendy as in Wendy Darling from *Peter Pan*. Uncle Will and my cousin Jake were named after Wilhelm and Jacob Grimm and my grandfather is the namesake of Charles Perrault, whom I'm sure you learned about when you read up on Cinderella."

No wonder Dylan rebelled in high school. He'd had enough of fairy tales.

"Don't forget Rory." Krystal gestured toward the grills. "That's Dylan's younger sister. Rory is short for Aurora. From *Sleeping Beauty*. Her brothers nicknamed her Rory and it stuck."

Jaine followed her finger toward a slender young woman glaring at Dylan with hands planted on her hips. Her glossy auburn fishtail braid dipped to an emerald green windbreaker with *All Star Dance Factory Staff* embroidered on the back. A yellow Lab panted at Dylan's feet, riveted on the cooking hotdogs.

"Tiara's given name fits her perfectly," Krystal continued. "She's adored glitter since kindergarten and has always wanted to make herself fancy like a tiara."

"I didn't realize you've known the Callahans that long, Krystal." Jaine didn't understand the look that passed between the two girls.

"I lived down the street from the inn with my grandmother. Tiara's mom watched me after school."

"Krystal's one of the family," Tiara said. "People thought we were sisters since she has a sparkly name, too. My parents called us Glitter and Glitz because Krystal always borrowed my makeup. Uh oh, speaking of family. . . ."

Rory Callahan stormed over to them, hands balled at her

sides. With her auburn hair and the light sprinkle of freckles dusting her cheeks, she bore no resemblance to Dylan except for her green eyes. Her dance windbreaker topped a pair of denim shorts that showed off her lithe athletic build.

"What's up, Cuz?" Tiara asked.

Rory gritted her teeth. "My overprotective big brother was bugging me about Brad not coming to the cookout. Dylan can't get it through his head that medical residents work long hours. His program is intense. That doesn't make him a lousy boyfriend."

"Dylan's looking out for his kid sister." Tiara planted her palms on the table, bracelets jingling on her wrist. "Don't be too hard on the guy."

"He's never dated a girl more than a month and has the nerve to imply *Brad* can't commit?"

Jaine slanted a casual glance in Dylan's direction. Their gazes collided and a slow grin spread across his face. She managed a small smile back.

Rory heaved a sigh. "Sorry, I shouldn't bring up family stuff at a company picnic, in front of new employees."

"This is Jaine, the marketing coordinator and replacement Cindy," Krystal said.

Jaine hoped Rory wasn't against an in-house marketing coordinator like her parents. "It's nice to meet you. I have two older sisters, so I can relate to annoying siblings."

Sorry, Dylan.

"Are your sisters always trying to protect you, or is that just an older brother thing?" Rory asked.

Jaine thought for a moment. Did the twins protect her? When they were kids, they never noticed her unless she volunteered to do their chores or lend her allowance. Jaine knew her sisters cared, but they got so immersed in their own lives, they forgot to show it.

"I'm the one looking out for them. They criticize though. I suppose that's their way of taking an interest."

"Dylan might be an annoying brother, but I must admit, he's a great general manager. Hiring you was a fantastic idea. We've worked with the same firm forever and their gimmicks are getting stale. Thanks for helping out with Cinderella." Rory smirked in her brother's direction. "Although it *was* funny seeing Dyl in a panicked state. My brother Jake and I kept texting him jokes about whether he'd caught Cinderella with a bong or Dazzle with a six-pack."

Jaine chuckled. She liked Rory. And Tiara. The Callahan women were a spirited bunch. "Do you work here, too?"

"I choreograph the shows and help out when they need me, but I spend most of my time teaching at a dance studio. Well, ladies, wish I could hang with you, but my mother is giving me the evil eye. I was on my way to get more hotdog rolls and coleslaw when Dylan distracted me."

Tiara waited until her cousin had left the table before smacking her forehead with her palm. Round citrine, garnet, and amethyst gemstones gleamed from her sterling silver bracelet. "When is she going to realize her boyfriend is a jerk?" she whispered. "Rory's brilliant about everything except men."

"So Dylan's right?" Jaine asked.

"Totally. I don't want her getting mad at me so I keep my mouth shut, but it's tough. I don't know if Krystal told you this, but we're all roommates. Rory, Krystal, Wendy, and I live in one of my parents' cabins. It's hard seeing Rory with a guy who's not good enough for her. She pretends it doesn't bother her, but we know it does."

"Brad thinks his stuff is more important than hers." Krystal touched a pack of Storybook Valley playing cards. "He never comes to her functions, but Rory goes to all his events. We get that he's busy, but if Brad really cared about her, he'd make more effort."

"Sounds like my sister's ex-husband. She didn't listen to us, either." Jaine forced herself to study the prizes and not her boss. She hoped Rory knew how lucky she was that her brother cared enough to tell her the truth.

Jaine picked up one of the blue Storybook Valley T-shirts and extended her sheet of gold stars to Tiara. "I'll take this."

Krystal handed her stars to Tiara and selected an envelope. "I'll grab these movie passes. See you later, T."

Jaine and Krystal loaded paper plates with hotdogs, potato chips, and coleslaw, and then headed to a picnic table. The crowd had thinned. Most teens and college students were in line for the rollercoaster and Ferris wheel, staffed by supervisors tonight. Soon after they sat down, Sean joined them. A polo shirt and khaki shorts replaced the Prince Charming costume.

"Hey, Jaine, do you know Gabrielle Allaire?" Sean squirted a packet of mustard onto his hotdog.

"Gabrielle Allaire?" Jaine's eyes enlarged behind her glasses. She hadn't heard that name in years. It didn't seem like long enough. "I went to school with her. Why?"

"That's what I figured. She was talking to Therese about you and mentioned seventh grade. You know Gabrielle works here, right?"

Jaine almost swallowed her relish-coated tongue. "What?"

"Gabrielle's the vice president of support staff. She gets to tell the administrative assistants what to do. There she is now." Krystal pointed to a young woman huddled with Therese. Sleek black hair rippled to her waist and a sleeveless black dress accented her perfect figure and tan.

Crap. It really *was* Gabrielle Allaire.

Krystal hunched forward, so close that Jaine caught the fragrance of her vanilla perfume. "Were you friends? Enemies? You can be honest. I never talk to her. She's too bossy for my taste."

Jaine pushed away her half-eaten hotdog, her appetite diminished. "Not friends. Not enemies, either. She was more of a frenemy. I lost to her in everything."

"Like what?"

"Grades, for one. She always scored a couple points higher than I did on tests. If I got a ninety-nine she got a hundred."

"A little competitive, aren't you?" Sean chuckled.

"Maybe a teensy bit," Jaine said. "But, those points counted when she was named valedictorian and I came in second, and when we applied for local scholarships. She won both scholarships."

They'd only amounted to $250 and $400, but Jaine had thought she'd had a chance. Losing to Gabrielle Allaire, not once, but twice, prickled.

"That sucks." Krystal sipped her bottled water. "Doesn't seem fair she won both."

"There's more. The newspaper advisor appointed Gabrielle editor-in-chief and me assistant editor. She got the highest score on the SATs in our class. Oh, and in a bout of insanity, I let my family talk me into running for class president and. . .drum roll. . .I lost to Gabrielle."

Krystal batted away a fly. "Be grateful. You avoided getting sentenced to class reunion hell, hoping that in your old age you'll be so senile that someone else will plan the reunions. It's not fun calling your classmates' parents to track down addresses and getting stuck social networking with people you hated."

"Let me guess. You're a class officer."

"Vice president. I got coerced into organizing a booze cruise. Making sure the guys didn't drown was less fun than a Pap smear, especially since the president was the biggest lush."

Sean's handsome face blanched. "A Pap smear? Do we need to go there?"

Despite her horror at seeing Gabrielle, Jaine's lips curled upward. She wondered if Dylan helped with the booze cruise since he had experience in that area. "Can't you tell them you moved to Wisconsin? Or Japan? Is this really a lifetime commitment?"

"Quiet, she's coming," Sean murmured.

Gabrielle threaded her way to the table, headed straight for Jaine. "I don't believe it. Jaine Andersen."

She lifted her arms for an embrace. Jaine had no choice but to rise and hug her.

"I heard Dylan charmed a new office assistant into playing Cinderella, but I've been away for a few days and didn't know the details. I didn't recognize you in the Cindy get-up."

Jaine manufactured a smile, wishing Sean could give her a few acting lessons. "What a coincidence. I didn't realize you worked here."

"I'll be your supervisor. Isn't that fab?" Gabrielle flipped her silky locks over her shoulder.

Jaine's stomach dropped. "I thought I was reporting to

Dylan."

"In the technical sense, but I'm in charge of the office staff's day-to-day operations. Therese and I were chatting about how you'll be in my territory. Poor Dylan, I guess he forgot to mention that. He's still learning how things work."

Adrenaline pitched through Jaine. This couldn't be true. She wanted to talk to Dylan *now*.

"We can discuss that later. Tonight the priority is giving our team an enjoyable event. It was wonderful running into you, Jaine."

"Watch your back with her," Krystal warned once Gabrielle departed. "She's Therese's prodigy, the daughter of a close friend. I love Therese, but she trusts Gabrielle a little too much."

"Believe me, I've always watched my back around Gabrielle." Jaine connected her clammy hands.

She was just settling into her Cinderella role, not thrilled, but making the best of it. Now she had to deal with Gabrielle Allaire?

"Didn't she used to go out with Dylan?" Sean asked.

"Briefly, during Gabrielle's second summer here," Krystal said. "Back when she was in college. He broke her heart."

Well, that was good news at least. Gabrielle had a higher-level job than Jaine. It wouldn't be fair if she nabbed the guy, too. Jaine busied herself with unwrapping a bag of potato chips while her companions continued talking.

"I've heard Dylan has broken a lot of hearts," Sean noted.

"That's for sure. I'd love to meet the girl who gets Dylan Callahan to settle down. He's been all business since taking over the park though. Wonder how long that will last."

Jaine's fingers tightened around the bag and her chips

crunched into smithereens. Dylan didn't kiss her because of a special connection. He would have trouble resisting any female left alone with him.

Dylan had shared his dating history, but hearing others discuss it made it seem more real.

And that made Jaine feel more stupid.

Chapter Seven

Around eleven o'clock, as co-workers spilled out the front gate, Jaine and Sean waited outside the bathroom for Krystal. Jaine scooped her keys from her purse.

"So Jaine, if you don't have a boyfriend, I was wondering if you'd consider going out sometime." Sean flashed a smile.

Whoa. First a stolen kiss with her boss, now Prince Charming hitting on her. Jaine had garnered more interest from men in the past two days than over the past six months.

Sean wasn't her boss, nor was he the owners' son, so a date *should* be okay. Besides, maybe a date with Prince Charming would help her forget her boss's kiss. Sean was cute and Jaine would never land a wedding date if she hibernated in her apartment.

Still. . .Dylan's parents might disapprove of their new Cinderella dating Prince Charming. Though Lois would likely consider it method acting and applaud her commitment to the role.

"I'd like to, but I'm a little hesitant because I'm new," Jaine admitted.

"It's allowed, and believe me, it happens all the time, but if you're more comfortable, let's not call it a date. Let's just go out as friends. Maybe we can catch a movie next Sunday night. You have that off, right?"

Jaine hadn't seen a movie in months. Relaxing in a plush theater chair sounded divine. Sean seemed like a nice guy and she deserved a night out.

She found herself nodding. "Okay. That sounds fun."

His face relaxed into another easy smile. "Great. We'll touch base when it gets closer."

Once Krystal returned, they exited through the front gate and Sean walked them to their cars. After he left, Krystal gave Jaine a questioning look. "Well? Did he ask you out?"

A brisk chill tinged the air and Jaine wrapped her arms around her Storybook Valley sweatshirt. Streetlights and headlights shone beneath the starry sky. "How did you know?"

"I could tell he was thinking about it from the way he was watching you. I went to the bathroom to give you privacy. You're welcome."

"We'd better consult next time. What if I didn't like him?"

"Do you?"

"Sure, but I don't think I'm ready to date a co-worker yet so we're just going out as friends." Jaine pressed the key pad to unlock her door, and the alarm blared. She must have hit the panic button.

"Oops." She fumbled with the button in the darkness. Krystal clapped her hands over her ears.

"I should have known it was you two causing such a commotion," a familiar voice said once the noise ceased.

Jaine spun to find Dylan grasping the leash of the yellow Lab she noticed earlier. Electricity zipped through her. Damn, why did he always have this effect on her? She couldn't decide which irked most, her internal reaction to Dylan's presence, his heartbreaker reputation, or that he forgot to tell her she would report to Gabrielle.

"Speaking of commotion, you got Rory all riled up." Krystal scratched behind the Lab's ear. "You should be more subtle about hating your sister's boyfriend. Otherwise she might keep dating him to prove a point."

"Someone's got to tell her the truth. Maybe if she hears it often enough, she'll quit lying to herself." Dylan's phone beeped, and he drew it out of his shorts pocket. He grinned and held up the screen. "It's a picture of my niece using the present I sent for her birthday."

Jaine's annoyance thawed at the image of a toddler atop a plush pink rocking horse. How could she stay mad at a guy who cared about his sister and bought his niece a pink rocking horse? "She's adorable, Dylan. What a cute gift."

Krystal intercepted the phone and stared. "Quinn got so big. Look at that. She's got Jake's eyes. And your impish smile. It still seems so weird that Jake's a daddy."

"When we went camping last month, he asked how you were doing," Dylan said. "You ought to call him."

Dark curls swinging, she shook her head and handed back the phone. "He doesn't have time for an old friend of his sister."

"You're family, Krystal. Of course he'll want to hear from you."

The Lab trotted over to Jaine and panted. She bent to stroke the dog's yellow coat. Its tail wagged gently at first then in a buoyant circular pattern. "Well, hello. What's your name?"

"It's Snow." Dylan texted a quick note back to his brother and pocketed the phone.

Jaine couldn't stay miffed at Dylan, but she could at least tease him. "How sweet. You named your dog after Snow

White." Squatting, she scratched under Snow's chin. The animal let out a contented bark.

"You're kidding, right? You think I'd name her after someone dumb enough to bite into a poisonous apple?"

"Must have been the Snow Queen then." Jaine petted Snow, the dog bouncing around her in exaggerated twists.

"Unlike my crazy family, I don't get inspiration from fairy tales. She and I both love snow. You know, the powdery stuff you've never used for skiing? The first day I got her, this girl rolled around in it." Snow pawed at his legs. Obeying the animal's request, Dylan crouched and rubbed under the dog's collar.

"I named my cat Willow. She's slender and graceful like the branches of a willow tree."

"Very poetic."

"I'd love to stay and chat about pets, but I'm exhausted. I'm calling it a night." Krystal unlocked the coupe beside Jaine's car.

"Me too. Thanks for coming tonight, ladies." Dylan gave Snow one more affectionate pat and stood. "You're wearing the sweatshirt. I knew I picked the right one."

Heat crept into Jaine's neck as she remembered Dylan's comment about her eyes. She swallowed, a wave of wistfulness churning through her. She had enjoyed this unexpected meeting. Jaine patted the dog once more and straightened.

"Thanks again. It's comfortable. See you guys later. Bye, Snow."

She climbed into her driver's seat, wishing for a five-minute drive instead of fifteen. Jaine chucked her purse and new T-shirt onto the floor and slid the key into the ignition.

Okay, she hadn't expected the Gabrielle thing, but she had

a promising new job and an upcoming sort-of date with Sean. Talking with Dylan after the kiss wasn't as awkward as she'd feared. Instead, it felt surprisingly natural. Jaine should be pumped with optimism.

Not drowning in doubt.

***

The next day, Jaine scanned the time clock in the front office. She greeted Therese, who was logging into her computer, with a polite hello. Therese sipped from a Storybook Valley coffee mug with steaming wisps curling past the rim.

Jaine never understood why people drank coffee on scorching days, but the rich fragrance triggered memories of the breakfast nook nestled in the corner of her childhood kitchen. Her parents enjoyed a cup every morning at the wood-planked table while sharing the newspaper. After her mother died, Jaine continued the tradition for her father except she drank juice if she wasn't in a coffee mood.

She wondered if he maintained the habit with Gloria. Jaine knew little about their routine, other than it revolved around Gloria's grandchildren. They babysat and shuttled the kids back and forth to preschool while Gloria's daughter worked.

Meanwhile, poor Amber hadn't hugged her grandfather in six months.

Therese lowered her mug to a spot beside her in-tray. "Dylan asked me to assign you a temporary desk."

"That would be great," Jaine responded.

Finally, a space of her own that didn't have turrets.

Therese pointed to a desk in the corner, near the copy machine. It held a computer, printer, telephone, and files organized into vertical bins. "You can work over there. One of our part-time administrative assistants uses it in the mornings, but it's free after one o'clock and on weekends."

Dylan sauntered into the room, munching a sugared apple cider doughnut from the bakery. "Just the princess I wanted to find. So? Did you see them?"

Jaine's forehead wrinkled. "See what?"

"Seriously? You didn't notice them in the sky?"

"Noooo." Jaine enunciated her words, as if she were speaking to someone slow on the uptake, even though in this case, perhaps she was the slow one. Dylan's mother seemed confused, too. Therese trained a puzzled gaze on her son.

"Funny," Dylan continued. "It's tough to miss three little pigs soaring over the park."

Their conversation in his office the other day rushed back to Jaine. She blinked a couple times. "No way! You're giving me the go-ahead?"

"For the Back-to-School Ball. We'll revisit the Halloween ball next year."

"But that's so easy to put together and we could promote it at the same time," Jaine objected, her enthusiasm catapulting her into full-blown marketing mode.

Dylan cast an eye-roll toward the ceiling. "I knew you would say that. We don't have the resources right now to concentrate on two big events. Besides, we'd be competing with a ton of other local Halloween happenings, so it would take lots of effort to make ours stand out."

And it might be stressful for her to coordinate such a challenge during her first few months on the job. Jaine's dad used to say that her eyes were bigger than her stomach. Maybe her eyes were also bigger than her time sheet.

"I didn't think about the competition. But I'll remind you to re-consider next year when I'll have more time to plan."

"I'm sure you will."

They both glanced up at the sound of a throat clearing. Gabrielle glowered at Dylan from the doorway, arms folded over the sleeveless black top of her pantsuit, and a Louis Vuitton handbag dangling over her shoulder. "I wish you would have consulted with me about this ball, Dylan."

"Why's that, Gabrielle?" He matched her cool tone.

"The front office is busy organizing the Employee Appreciation Cookout. I could use Jaine's help. We need to design the invitations, coordinate with the catering staff, and print out the certificates, not to mention speak with all the supervisors so we can get their award nominations. It's a huge undertaking."

Dylan's eyebrows arched. "You have the entire support staff to help you. Why do you need my marketing coordinator?"

"This is an internal public relations project. If you want our best employees to return next season, then we need to plan a successful event."

"If we want to attract more customers, then we need to focus on external campaigns. I'm sure you'll put together a fantastic event, Gabrielle. But you'll do it without Jaine. She's not part of your support staff."

Gabrielle's cheeks flushed red. Jaine worked hard to keep her face neutral. This was astounding. No one had ever pulled rank on Gabrielle Allaire. Where was the trumpet salute?

Therese spoke up from her desk. "Dylan, you were impulsive about creating this position. You didn't consult with any of us. I can understand why Gabrielle is confused about the job description."

"The general manager shouldn't need to consult with anyone." Dylan's voice sharpened.

Now things were getting awkward. Jaine checked her watch. "If you'll excuse me, my shift starts soon."

"We don't want to hold you up from your most *important* role." Gabrielle gave a dry laugh. "What was I thinking? Jaine doesn't have time to help with the appreciation event, and Dylan, if I were you I would reconsider this back-to-school thing. Jaine needs to put her effort into Cinderella if we're going to convince these kids she's the real deal. An *ordinary* girl trying to transform into a princess is a full-time job."

"How nice of you to be concerned, Gabrielle, but I'll be fine. I'm used to multi-tasking. Excuse me." Jaine brushed past her former classmate and fled out the door. She hadn't missed the emphasis on ordinary.

Releasing a long puff of air, Jaine slumped against the building's clapboard siding. Dylan had rescued her, but in the process he'd infuriated Gabrielle. That didn't bode well for a smooth work relationship between her and Jaine.

Dylan appeared behind her and motioned for Jaine to follow. He strode a few feet toward the wardrobe cottage and faced her. "I wanted to get out of earshot. Sorry about the thing with Gabrielle. I heard you two went to school together."

"We were rivals even though she always won."

"She was angling for the general manager job before I showed up. My parents were considering training her until I came home and ruined her plan." Dylan sent Jaine a wry glance. "There might be one other reason she hates me, too."

Jaine tilted her head. "Your reputation precedes you. Could it be because Gabrielle was one of the girls in your little black book and you shattered her heart?"

Dylan groaned. "Who told you that? My cousin or sister?"

"Krystal."

"Same thing. They all live together so she's practically another cousin. First of all, I don't have a little black book. I keep contacts on my cell phone." He dug his black cell out of his pocket and showed it to her. "See?"

"Duly noted. Gabrielle was one of the many women in your little black phone." Jaine nodded solemnly. Teasing a boss wasn't like her, but Dylan ignited her sense of humor. Kissing her boss wasn't like Jaine either. . .humor wasn't the only side Dylan kindled.

"*Anyway*, I was nice about it, but she kept texting and calling. She must have sent twenty texts saying how much she missed me. I responded that we could still be friends, but that was all, and then I stopped returning her messages. She sent one telling me what a jerk I was. Gabrielle's given me the cold shoulder ever since."

They resumed their walk and Jaine commented, "She must be upset you had the power to hire me. Though she seems pretty smug that she's in a management role and I'm in a Cinderella gown."

"She's just jealous because she knows I'd cast her as a villain."

Could Gabrielle really envy Jaine for portraying a beautiful princess? Nah. She'd prefer to keep Jaine exiled in the castle, signing autographs, forever. Ugh.

That horrible thought spurred Jaine to ask, "Can you give me a list of your local media contacts? We're throwing this together at the last minute so it will help if I sent the press release to the right people."

"My dad handled the media. The ads we're running now are ones he set up awhile ago. I planned to transfer those responsibilities to you."

"Do you think your father would chat with me?"

Jaine and Dylan paused outside the door of the pink wardrobe cottage. The fragrance of roses wafted through the air and birds twittered overhead. In a few hours, the humidity would send visitors rushing to the water rides, but Jaine enjoyed the early morning warmth. Despite the peaceful setting, she bit her lower lip at the prospect of asking the imposing Will Callahan for a favor.

Dylan sighed. "I don't think that's a good idea. I can't see him supporting the Back-to-School Ball. We have different opinions of where to budget money. You should have seen his reaction when I switched to cheaper paper towels in the bathrooms."

"Cheaper paper towels. How dare you," Jaine chided.

"Yeah, I'm a real tightwad. Except for when I hire useless marketing coordinators. Then I'm careless." Dylan bumped her with his shoulder and a tingle darted up her spine.

"You're still a penny-pincher. Who the hell makes their marketing person dress up as Cinderella?"

"A creative thinker?"

"That's one way to put it. Seriously, though, you're always here. I'm sure your dad appreciates that." Jaine fought the urge to lay a comforting hand on his bare muscled arm.

"Maybe, but I don't want to take the chance that he'll be rude." Dylan shook his head. "How about you speak to my grandfather? He'll be flattered to give you advice. In fact, I bounced your back-to-school idea off Granddad and he was all for it."

"When's the best time to approach him? I'll visit him on my day off."

"He has a drink at Castle Cookery around four o'clock. He spends his break having a soda and moving gnomes."

"Moving *what*?"

Dylan rubbed the back of his neck. "You'll see. Unfortunately. Don't be surprised if he asks you to help. In case you haven't noticed, my family's nuts."

Jaine closed her fingers around the doorknob. She wished that she and Dylan could talk longer, but children would race into the park soon and she still looked like a Plain Jaine. "Okay then. I'll join your granddad for a drink and gnomes. I'll send drafts of my press release and flyer soon."

"Don't work from home since we need you to clock in and out. I'll have my cousin Cas set up your email account and computer login. Save your work on our company's internal hard drive, the K Drive. And one more thing." Dylan sketched a bow. "Have a good day, Your Highness."

"Hmm, I like that. I think you should bow all the time."

His cheeks dimpled. "Yeah, that ain't gonna happen. See you later."

As Dylan left, Jaine stepped into the air conditioning of the now familiar wardrobe department. She itched to put on her marketing hat and dig into her project, but alas, for the next several hours, she was stuck wearing a tiara.

Chapter Eight

Jaine spent Sunday, her first day off from work, watching the 1953 romantic comedy *Roman Holiday* on DVD. No wonder Audrey Hepburn's performance landed her the Academy Award for Best Actress. She did a fantastic job portraying the runaway Princess Ann who rebels against her sheltered life and falls in love with an American newspaperman, portrayed by Gregory Peck. Sort of Cinderella in reverse.

As the end credits rolled, Jaine switched off the television and tossed the remote control onto the coffee table. She had enjoyed the film, but the movie didn't teach her how to act royal. Instead, it reminded her she was no Audrey Hepburn. Not even close.

But one person had viewed her as a princess for her whole life. Her father. Her dad had forwarded a couple joke emails, but she hadn't talked to him in two weeks. He hadn't even heard about her new career move. Jaine sat down at the kitchen table and called him.

"Good job, honey," her father applauded a few minutes later. "You saw an opportunity, went for it, and they created a whole job around your skills. That's terrific."

"Thanks, Dad. I'm excited." She had left out the Cinderella duties. Her dad would understand her reasons for accepting the position, but Jaine's stepmother, a retired high school principal, wouldn't get it.

Besides, he might slip up and mention it in front of Jaine's sisters during the wedding activities. The twins would brainstorm an infinite supply of Cinderella jokes. Bree would be at her firstborn's high school graduation, teasing Jaine about glass slippers.

"You sound busy," her father said. "Make sure you don't take on too many wedding errands. Bree doesn't need to work sixty hours per week."

"I'd feel guilty if I didn't help. She's so stressed."

"That's fine, just don't make yourself exhausted. You have a habit of always putting other people's needs before your own. You're important too, Jaine."

Her father had the same habit. When her dad started dating Gloria, a woman he met at a library book club, Jaine approved of his new companion. They seemed casual, going out to an occasional dinner or movie. Jaine met Gloria a few times, to exchange a quick hello, and didn't know her well enough to form a strong like or dislike. Then after a few months, Gloria's son-in-law transferred to Tallahassee. Suddenly Jaine's father was planning a City Hall wedding, selling the house, and moving to Florida with this stranger.

"I'll keep that in mind." Jaine toyed with an apple in her fruit bowl.

"I called the hotel's wedding coordinator, the florist, the photographer, and the videographer to make sure the financial details are squared away, so you girls shouldn't worry about any of that."

Although their dad wasn't around to take an active part in the wedding plans, he was paying and helping the best he could from Florida. "Thanks, Dad."

"How's my granddaughter doing? I can't tell you how much I miss that kid."

"She's eight-going-on thirteen. Very into music and tween shows on the Disney Channel."

"Can't wait to see all of you. I miss you kids." A note of sadness tinged his voice.

Then you shouldn't have moved to Florida. But Jaine didn't speak the accusation out loud.

"Looking forward to seeing you too, Dad. Love you." Jaine disconnected.

At least her father had found someone, but she would prefer a woman who lived in New York.

As Willow nuzzled her ankle, Jaine bent to caress her cat. Then she went into her bedroom closet, dragged out her stuffed hamper, and located the large plastic bin crammed with her mother's scrapbooks.

Jaine knelt on the carpet and leafed through the bound albums while Willow sniffed around the bin. She flipped the pages of book-after-book, brushing her fingertips against the bright backgrounds. Her mom had loved buying scrapbooking supplies. Glitter paper, chalkboard paper, floral patterns, holiday-themed card stock, decorative stickers. She created special scrapbooks for school memories, birthdays, and vacations, along with an album devoted to each daughter.

A lump lodged in Jaine's throat when she found the Storybook Valley photographs. In elegant silver cursive her mother had written "Royal Days with Our Princesses." She'd mounted tiara, castle, and wand decals onto the violet pages, interspersed with pictures of the girls riding the carousel, antique cars, and flying slippers.

Jaine's chest tightened at the photograph of her mom, the twins, and herself gathered around Cinderella's throne. Jaine had been six then and while the twins weren't overly eager to greet Cinderella, they were young enough to enjoy the theme park without complaining. In the picture, Jaine beamed at Cinderella in awe.

She had once considered Cinderella stunning, before Jaine learned the gold hair was a wig, the magnificent gown had several matches hanging on a rack, and the damn shoes caused blisters.

Tears blurring her vision, she carried the album to her bed and sat cross-legged on her patchwork quilt. Jaine spread the book across her lap and fingered her mother's careful script, wanting nothing more than to relive the days when fairy tales were real and her family was whole.

***

On Monday, her second day off, Jaine drove to Storybook Valley in the late afternoon and sought out Dylan's grandfather. When Jaine reached Castle Cookery, she discovered Charles Callahan seated alone at a table along the perimeter. Since it was past lunch and too early for dinner, only a handful of families scattered the other tables, escaping the sunlight for a snack break. Teen workers wiped counters and replenished condiment bins.

Mr. Callahan sipped a Sprite and crunched from a box of popcorn. As she neared his table, a toothy grin deepened the crevices of his face. He tipped his engineer cap, which covered unruly grey hair. "Well, hello there, Jaine. I've been meaning to welcome you to our team."

"Thank you. It's wonderful to meet you, Mr. Callahan. May I join you?"

He gestured toward a ceramic garden gnome on the stone bench opposite him. "Call me Charles. Have a seat next to Filfinkle Finebang."

"Um. . .who?" Jaine regarded the faded gnome with its white bristle poking out from under a pointy green hat and a gigantic smile lighting red lips. Bushy brows crowned closed eyes and a bulbous nose popped out of the bearded face.

That's right. Dylan had mentioned this little quirk. Jaine perched beside Filfinkle Finebang.

"I'm a garden gnome liberationist," Charles said. "Perhaps you've heard of us. We advocate for the freedom of gnomes. Don't you think they must get awfully bored trapped in the same gardens all the time?" His sea foam eyes twinkled beneath thick glasses.

Garden gnome liberationists? Was that a thing?

Jaine matched his tongue-in-cheek tone. "I never considered that. I suppose you're right, they must get bored. What does a garden gnome liberationist do?"

"Every day I move one or two gnomes to a different location. I even put the gnomes on rides and post pictures around the park." Charles leaned forward, pressing his gaunt arms against the table.

"But my favorite liberating act was kidnapping Elthink Puddlesteel, a gnome from Duke's Animal World, and taking him on a trip out west. Afterwards, I returned him with an album of pictures from Yellowstone National Park, the Grand Canyon, Las Vegas, Hollywood, and the Golden Gate Bridge."

"Wow! That's amazing. Were the zoo's owners excited?"

Jaine made a mental note to tell Dylan how awesome his grandfather was. Charles reminded her how much she missed her own grandparents. Her maternal grandparents had died several years earlier and her dad's parents lived in New Hampshire.

"That old bastard, Duke Thorne, called the police. But you don't want to hear all that. What can I do for you, my dear?"

"I'd love to pick your brain about local media contacts, to find out which reporters and editors I can trust with our coverage requests and which ones to avoid."

"I'm honored. No one asks my advice anymore, except for Dylan. You'll have a list of names tomorrow."

"Thank you so much."

"I'm counting on you and Dylan to make us more popular than Duke's Animal World. You and I will have to chat sometime about their new camp program." Charles Callahan eyed his vintage watch, gold-filled with a tarnished face. "For now, might you grant me a favor, Jaine? Our little friend Filfinkle needs another location."

Great. He wanted her to move the gnome. Jaine slanted an uncertain look at Filfinkle Bangshebang, or whatever its name was. "Um, sure. Where should I put him?"

"Anywhere you want. Except for the flower garden at the front entrance. He's already been there for a week." Rising, Charles winked at Jaine. "Best of luck with your new position, my dear. If you'll excuse me, I need to return to the train."

"I'll walk you out."

Once they separated a few moments later, Jaine eyeballed the cheerful gnome clutched to her waist. She had to unload this thing as quickly as possible. Jaine decided on the pond where she and Dylan had shared lemonade. . .and more.

She'd seen fluffy golden yellow flowers blooming and even a garden gnome or two. Jaine headed in that direction, passing a rollaway cart selling hair wreaths and cone-shaped princess hats shimmering with sequins and gemstones. She sidestepped the families lined up at the frozen dessert cart.

"Hello, Jaine."

Jaine closed her eyes for a second and then swung around to face Gabrielle. "Hey. What's up?"

Gabrielle tapped the clipboard pressed to her sleeveless plum pantsuit. With her glossy black hair woven into a perfect French braid, she looked cool and crisp despite the humidity. "How nice to run into you. I was just out doing errands."

She cocked her head toward Filfinkle. Rounded topaz earrings gleamed from behind her dark wisps of hair. "My, Dylan is making impressive use of your talents. Liberating gnomes is *such* an important part of theme park marketing."

Sweat moistened Jaine's forehead, not to mention her armpits. She wondered which stressor had fried her internal temperature: the heat itself, the statue's weight, Gabrielle's sarcasm, or the shame of hefting a bearded elf before Ms. Perfect. Most likely, A, B, C, and D.

"I'm doing a favor for Charles."

"That's kind of you to fit it into your schedule. Since Dylan insists you're so busy." Gabrielle spoke in a sugary voice, but Jaine caught the bitter flash in her eyes.

"Yes, well, I'd better go." Jaine shifted the gnome in her hands. "Lots to do. Have a nice afternoon."

"Have fun being a gnome freedom fighter." Gabrielle strolled past Jaine, her lips fixed in a tight smile.

Could Jaine get fired for clocking a witch with a dwarf?

Yeah, probably. She adjusted her grip around Filfinkle Boomshebang. . .or something like that. . . and continued on her mission.

Chapter Nine

The next morning, Jaine swept into the castle in her ball gown, ready for another day of the Cinderella grind. She had twenty minutes of peace before the park opened and parents descended with their cameras and children. Jaine spotted a green-shirted gnome on her throne, a white sheet of notebook paper underneath his coal black boots. He stared straight ahead through big eyes, arms spread at the sides.

She drew out the paper. A note topped columns of hand-written names and phone numbers. *Pithmink Puddlesprocket was nice enough to deliver my promised media contacts. He would love to spend time on the castle grounds. Sincerely, Charles.*

Perfect timing. After their conversation yesterday, Jaine had typed a draft press release, designed a flyer, and emailed them to Dylan for his review.

Slosh, slosh. What the heck was that? Jaine approached the bathroom door. "Hello?"

She peeked inside to discover Dylan with his hand plunged into the toilet tank.

He winked at her. "Told you I'd fix it. We can't have Cinderella using a running toilet. It ruins the castle ambiance."

Oh God, were they back to the toilet again?

"Thanks," Jaine replied without enthusiasm.

"I mean, princesses deserve a royal throne wherever they sit."

"Okay! Let's talk about something else. Once you approve the press release, I'll send it out to the papers. When it gets closer to the event, I'll follow up to remind them that we invited a reporter and photographer. By the way, I love your grandfather. That garden gnome thing is hysterical."

"He got into that a few years ago." Dylan returned to his repairs. "My parents worried it was a sign of dementia, but he was just bored. He misses the day-to-day managing of the park."

"It's nice that you ask for his advice. I looked up the liberation movement on the Internet. I didn't realize people did that. By the way, what's the deal with your grandfather and the guy from Duke's Animal World? I got the impression they dislike each other."

"They were friends growing up, and then had some kind of falling out. When they opened competing businesses, things got even worse. Their kids hate each other, too. Pretty immature, huh?"

Actually, Jaine could relate. She wouldn't want her children hanging out with Gabrielle's twisted offspring.

"Hi, Jaine," a familiar male voice interrupted from behind them.

She pivoted toward the palace entrance, gown swishing. Sean had joined them in a park-issued shirt and shorts. With his slender build, he didn't fill out the shirt in the same rugged way that Dylan did, but he possessed definite Hollywood heartthrob potential.

"Sean, hi. I didn't expect to see you."

"I picked up extra hours working as a breaker, filling in

for people on their breaks. Someone's coming in late so I'm helping out at the Sky Ride. I figured you could check out Sunday's schedule." He showed her the list of movies on his cell phone.

She registered the name of the theater. "The drive-in?"

Jaine hoped he wasn't counting on a make-out session in the back seat. She wasn't a make-out-on-the-first-date kind of girl. Except for the Dylan incident, but that wasn't a date, it was a fluke.

Dylan. Jaine bit down on her newly applied lipstick. She wished this conversation wasn't unfolding in front of him. Not that it should matter, since they'd disregarded the kiss, but he was her boss. Besides, Jaine didn't want him thinking she flirted with every guy she met.

"We can catch two movies that way," Sean added. "Plus, they've got an epic snack bar. Do you like tacos? They've got killer tacos and enchiladas. Unless you'd prefer a regular theater."

No guy that enthusiastic about enchiladas could be contemplating heavy-duty kissing. Jaine darted a glance into the bathroom. Dylan worked in silence. "It sounds fun. I haven't been to a drive-in since I was a kid."

"They have screens with romantic comedies and action. You can pick."

"Thanks, that's nice of you to let me choose." Most of the guys she had dated planned outings without soliciting her input. Jaine pretended to like football and frat parties, but she tired of the same old thing every weekend.

Something clanked in the bathroom. Dylan had replaced the tank lid.

Sean peered over Jaine's shoulder. "Oh, hey, Dylan."

"Hey." Dylan folded his arms across his chest. "It's getting late. You'd better head over to the Sky Ride."

"Right. See you later, Jaine."

"Thanks for coming by."

Once they were alone, Dylan flushed the toilet and washed his hands. He dried them on a paper towel. "I put in a new flapper. That should help. I'll hang out for a few minutes to make sure."

He joined Jaine outside the bathroom and they waited while the toilet did its thing. "So you're going on a date with Sean?"

"It's not a date. We're just going out as friends."

"To the drive-in? It's a date." Dylan clapped a hand against the wall.

"No, it isn't. We're getting to know each other. Don't you want your Cinderella and Prince Charming to have camaraderie?"

Dylan leveled his gaze at her. "If I wanted camaraderie, I'd go somewhere a lot nicer than a drive-in."

"Like where?" Her breathing quickened.

"I'd take her on a picnic to a secluded spot and have champagne and chocolate-covered strawberries for dessert. Then a sunset horseback ride."

Jaine pictured herself kissing Dylan on a luxurious blanket, tasting champagne on his lips. Her heart shivered. "How many times have you done that?"

"Never. I'm saving it for someone special."

A rush of adrenaline shot through Jaine's stomach. As the flushing toilet faded into silence, neither of them spoke. Jaine forced her awareness off Dylan and onto the elf occupying her throne.

"Um. . .on your way out could you set Pithmink Puddle-sprocket in front of the castle?" There was no better mood-killer than a name like Pithmink Puddlesprocket.

"Sure. I have a favor for you, too. After the park closes, would you mind hanging out here in costume for an extra fifteen minutes? There's someone I want you to meet."

***

At six o'clock, Jaine waited in the castle for Dylan despite her fatigue. A group of annoying teens had tried to cajole her into singing and Jaine lied that her throat was dry. Luckily a line formed and she got rid of them. Jaine much preferred younger kids, except for the ones that gnawed their pen. She'd lost count of how many sticky pens she handled in a day. Plus, her feet *ached* from these damn glass slippers.

Jaine heard Dylan's deep voice outside and a sizzle of awareness zinged through her. Okay, she could tolerate the shoes for a little while longer.

Dylan's sister, Rory, popped in first. Her hair streamed in a ponytail down the back of her purple top. A towheaded boy of about five zoomed forward on a power wheelchair, Dylan bringing up the rear. The boy huddled on an animal print seat, fingering the plush body of a stuffed lion armrest cover. He coasted to a stop in front of Jaine.

"Noah's here for his private story time." Dylan squatted beside the boy. "What story do you feel like today, kiddo?"

"Hmmm." Noah pressed a finger to his lips. "*Jack and the Beanstalk?*"

"Good choice! I'll look for it." Rory approached the birch bookcase behind the throne and knelt to study the spines.

Jaine shifted into Cinderella mode. "Thank you so much for visiting me, Noah. I love all the animals on your chariot." She joined Dylan on the floor and adjusted the infinite folds of her dress. She patted the stuffed lion's ruff. "Lions are my favorite creature in the entire kingdom. Are they your favorite, too?"

Noah shook his head.

"No? Then what's your favorite?"

"Giraffes." Noah giggled.

"Giraffes! My goodness, those are so tall! They're almost taller than Jack's beanstalk." Jaine accepted a hardcover picture book from Rory, who dropped into a cross-legged position beside the wheelchair.

Over the next few minutes, Jaine read the story aloud with Noah turning the pages. At first, she wished Dylan and his sister weren't listening, but after a few minutes, her inhibitions faded. Once she finished reading, Jaine closed the book and glanced at her audience. She caught Dylan watching her, and her heart did a somersault.

Rory looked from Jaine to her brother and a slight smile tugged her pink lips. She hopped to her feet. "Thank you, Cinderella. It's time to visit Red Riding Hood, right, Dyl?"

"Right. Ready, buddy?"

"Thank you, Cinderella." Noah scooted forward in his chair.

"Yeah, thanks, Cinderella." Dylan clasped Jaine's forearm for a few seconds, just long enough for her nerve endings to stir, and then stood to his full height. He reached down and helped her up off the floor, and once again Jaine tingled at his touch. She quickly released his hand.

Rory hung back as her brother and Noah left the castle.

"Thanks, Jaine. You did a great job with him. That meant a lot to Noah."

"He's a darling. How do you know him?" Jane moved over to a bench against the wall. She plopped onto the red velvet cushion and peeled off her shoes. Her feet needed a breather before she made the hike to Wardrobe.

Ah. Jaine exhaled. Much better.

"Our families are close friends, and they're season passholders. When they visit, Tiara, Dylan, or I give Noah VIP treatment while his parents go on fast rides with the older kids. Dylan's keeping the water slides open for them an extra hour tonight so they don't have to wait in line."

"That's so nice of him." Unfortunately, the gesture made her like Dylan even more. Jaine crossed an ankle over her gown and massaged her throbbing heel. At least the discomfort distracted her.

Rory unzipped a quilted white purse embroidered with roses. She slipped a business card out of her wallet and passed it to Jaine. "My brother asked me to choreograph the Back-to-School Ball. Why don't you send me the song list, or we can schedule a brainstorming session. I jotted my direct email on the back."

"That would be great. Thanks." Jaine examined the card. Silver sequins glimmered against a gold linen background. *All Star Dance Factory. . .Where We Make Dancers Shine* read the tagline. "Dylan mentioned that you were a dancer. It must be fun doing something you love."

Rory didn't answer right away, and Jaine wondered about her pensive expression. "Choreographing your show will be a nice change of pace." She pointed at Jaine's shoes, her fingernails gleaming with lilac polish. "Did Krystal mention the flip flops?"

"Flip flops? No."

"She was probably afraid to tick off my grandmother. I filled in for Cinderella a few times in high school." Rory adopted a dramatic stage whisper. "When no guests are around and you're on break, put on a pair of flip flops."

Now they tell me.

Chapter Ten

Jaine shifted in the passenger-side seat of Sean's car, balancing a Styrofoam plate in her lap. Every time she wanted a bite of her overstuffed taco, she had to hold the plate closer to her lips with her right hand and lift the taco with the left, leading to cheddar cheese flecks and salsa dribbles marring her favorite blouse, the silk one with swirling shades of cocoa brown, pink, and cream. Jaine squinted in the darkness, but couldn't tell whether the salsa landed on brown or cream.

"Aren't these tacos the best?" Sean asked from the driver's seat.

"They're delicious," she said with false cheeriness and blotted a napkin across her blouse, hoping the stain wouldn't set even more. These napkins were thinner than Dylan's cheap paper towels in the Storybook Valley bathrooms.

Poor Sean was working so hard to make this a fun date and Jaine could only think of Dylan, who would have teased her about the lack of taco-handling skills. After she retorted with a snappy comeback, Dylan would help her scrub the stain. Sean would assist too, but that prospect didn't elicit the same goosebumps.

She was fantasizing about Dylan, not Sean, leaning in close for a long kiss. . . .

Jaine shivered, not a brilliant idea with a taco on your lap.

118

"You okay?" Sean lowered the volume of the radio channel that delivered the movie's audio.

"Um, yeah. I thought I felt a mosquito." Jaine nodded toward her window, cracked open a few inches to let in a dash of air.

"I can close it."

What a cute and thoughtful guy. Why couldn't Sean be the one who triggered her goosebumps? "I'm all right. I think it was just my imagination."

Even if Dylan *had* seemed jealous about her going out with Sean, he was forbidden. Jaine watched the previews on the movie screen. The second film would start in a few moments. She needn't have worried about Sean getting frisky. Hundreds of cars lined the grass, and with the snack bar a few feet away, this section offered little privacy.

"How do you like playing a princess?" Sean asked.

"It's fine, but I'm no Audrey Hepburn."

"I view it as improv theater. Want some advice?" He paused from eating his third taco.

"Please!"

"Have fun with it. Don't worry about acting or thinking of clever things to say. Listen to what your visitors are saying and *react*. Connect to the other players. Tell kids that if they speak to Prince Charming, they should give him a message from you."

"What type of message?"

"Hmmm. . .you could say he looks amazingly handsome today." Sean grinned, showing those dazzling teeth.

Jaine laughed. Being with Sean was easy. . .just not exciting.

Once the second feature started, Jaine stifled a yawn. After her long week, she yearned to crawl into bed with Willow curled beside her.

She cradled her neck against the headrest, eyelids dragging to half-mast. She would just close her eyes for a minute. Sean would never know. . . .

"Jaine. Jaine."

Her eyes snapped open. Jaine's surroundings ebbed into focus. Slouching in her seat, she blinked at the shadowed view out the front window. Where was the movie screen? The rows of cars?

Jaine straightened her glasses on her nose. Was that her apartment building hulking in the shadows? She bolted straight up.

"Oh, my God! I fell asleep! I missed the whole movie, didn't I?"

Sean clicked off the ignition. "It wasn't that great anyway. The book that inspired it was better. I can see why it didn't grab you."

"Still, I'm so sorry. I can't believe I nodded off."

"No biggie. You must have been exhausted."

Jaine pinned her arms against her stomach. Who dozed off during first date? Sure, a girl might zone out while watching TV with her boyfriend, especially if it was something boring like golf, but after attaining a certain comfort level. Not on a first date.

Well, this wasn't technically a date. Ah, hell. Dylan was right. They'd gone to the drive-in and Sean paid. It was a date.

"Come on, I'll walk you to your place." Sean pocketed his keys.

They closed the doors to his Chevrolet. He had parked before the correct building, an impressive accomplishment at night since the dozen brick buildings in the complex looked alike.

Jaine stopped before the cement staircase leading to her front door. She gulped. Did he intend to kiss her? Did she want that?

"Well, thank you. I had a nice time."

"Me too." Sean hesitated under the moonlight and the faint glow from the streetlight.

Ugh. Jaine hated awkward moments. She was about to end the silence and say good night when he slanted forward and maneuvered his lips against hers in a rubbery kiss.

After the longest thirty seconds in history, Sean stepped back with a smile. Evidently, he relished the kiss more than she did, which mystified Jaine. Hadn't he sensed the missing chemistry? Didn't she have bad breath from the taco and falling asleep?

"Can I call you next weekend?" Sean asked.

Jaine couldn't wait to wipe saliva off her mouth. She must be the most ungrateful Cinderella on the planet. Other women would love the chance to date a gorgeous and considerate guy like Sean.

But, was it fair to string him along when they shared no sparks? A lackluster kiss was a lackluster kiss.

"The thing is I'm planning my sister's bachelorette party. It's next weekend and will be a late night. And then—"

"You'll go home and crash and turn into Sleeping Beauty again. I can take a rain check." Sean departed into the shadows with one last wave and Jaine rubbed a hand over her face.

She unlocked the front door and trekked up two flights to

her apartment. Jaine wanted to fall for Sean, but it wasn't happening. Maybe he would get the hint. They could be friends instead. She'd love to have him for a friend.

But, Sean thrived on challenges. Actors needed determination to drag themselves to audition-after-audition.

What if he didn't give up?

Chapter Eleven

The following afternoon, Jaine searched the mall for a killer bachelorette party dress. She'd skip the dinner, but there would be plenty of time after work to bar-hop with the girls. Her trilling cell phone interrupted an inner debate over whether to add a slinky black dress to her cart. May as well try it on.

Jaine draped it atop a sequined red dress and yanked her phone out of her purse. Krystal's number showed as the incoming caller. "Hi."

"You never told me how the date went," Krystal accused.

"It was okay." Jaine wheeled her cart away from the other customers shopping for formal wear and parked it in a secluded spot against the department store's back wall.

"Just okay?"

"Sean's such a nice guy, it's just that there's no chemistry."

"How much chemistry do you expect on a first date?"

"Enough to have sparks during the good night kiss. Plus, I fell asleep. I can't imagine falling asleep if I was out with. . ." Jaine caught herself before Dylan's name left her lips. "With someone I was attracted to."

"But you'll keep dating Sean, right?" Krystal asked. "Then you can invite him to the wedding."

"I don't want to lead him on just so I can use him for a

wedding date. That's not fair."

"I doubt Sean is looking for anything serious, Jaine. He told me it's his last summer in the Catskills, so he's heading somewhere, I'm not sure where. There's nothing wrong with having fun together. Unless the date was that bad?"

"We'll see what happens. I'd better go. I'm in line. Talk to you later."

Jaine shoved her cell back into her purse. Krystal wouldn't understand. Her sisters and other friends didn't, insisting she was too picky.

She pushed her cart toward the dressing rooms in the middle of the store. Cinderella had it so easy when compared to her fairy tale counterparts. She hadn't gotten locked in a tower, slept a hundred years, or eaten a poisoned apple. Tolerating a mean stepmother and stepsisters was a small expense for finding her prince.

I'm Cinderella. Why can't it be easy for me?

Ten minutes later, Jaine regarded her reflection in the rectangular mirror. The black dress swallowed her figure rather than fitting glove-like as she had hoped. Sighing, she crossed back toward the curtained dressing cubicle, past a matronly employee gathering garments from vacant stalls. Maybe she should give up and wear something out of her closet. Jaine had promised Shauna to pick up groceries and babysit Amber tonight.

"Might I make a suggestion?" The woman paused with a pile of designer bathing suit in her arms.

"Please do." Jaine nodded.

"I have a dress that will look gorgeous on you. If you can stay a moment, I'll be right back."

"Sure, thank you."

The salesperson hurried out to the women's department. Jaine settled on a bench to wait even though this one would likely disappoint, too.

A few moments later, the woman reappeared bearing a silk sheath, its rich aquamarine shade vibrant in the stark dressing chamber. She held up the price tag. "Try this. It was on a clearance rack."

Stunning and a mere $25?

"It's beautiful! Let's cross our fingers that it fits." Jaine carried the sheath behind the curtain and pulled off the shapeless black frock.

She slipped the luxurious silk over her head, smoothed the fabric around her waist, and inspected the results in the dimly lit mirror. This was her party dress! At least, she thought so. Such a monumental decision warranted a second opinion and more light.

"What do you think?" the woman called.

Jaine opened the curtain. The woman's loud gasp confirmed her suspicions that THIS WAS THE DRESS.

"I love it! It was made for you."

Hardly daring to breathe, Jaine edged past her admirer and twirled before the tall mirror. The sheath flattered her from the front, and she adored the pleats setting off the V-neckline in the back. Her sexy elegance would impress her sisters and maybe, just maybe, attract a Prince Charming.

Er, a Prince Charming besides Sean. Or Dylan.

Not bad for $25!

"I can't thank you enough for your help. You're like my fairy godmother."

"I'm so glad you think so. I saw the perfect rhinestone jewelry set in the jewelry department, with a glimmer of teal.

Best of all, it's on clearance, too."

Twenty minutes later, Jaine signed the credit card receipt for the dress and accessories. The young female cashier flicked a glance at it, wrinkled her nose, and drew it closer. She regarded Jaine with a bemused expression. "So how was traffic riding in a pumpkin coach?"

"What?" Jaine inspected her loopy cursive. Oops. It spelled out Cinderella. Lucky her, she'd gotten the one cashier who read signatures. She tugged at her collar. "I can explain."

***

In between playing princess, Jaine spent the week wrapping up the final bachelorette party details. She confirmed the limo, made reservations at an upscale French bistro for dinner and an elegant restaurant for brunch, decided on the nightclub itinerary, sent reminder emails to Bree's friends, and rented a romantic comedy DVD for the slumber party.

She also spent several hours in the front office. Her morning deskmate adored dogs judging from the cocker spaniel photograph taped to the computer monitor and the screen saver of a dozen pink-ribboned poodles. Jaine wondered how the woman would react to a picture of Willow the cat.

Jaine set up a media contact database, emailed the approved press release and calendar listing to area newspapers, photocopied the flyers, and left the stack on Dylan's chair for distribution. (Since they would get lost on his desk.) Dylan would have a staff member deliver piles to Guest Relations and the ticket booths and hang the rest around the park.

Saturday night after the fireworks, Jaine unloaded her

locker in the wardrobe department, spreading high-heeled black sandals, jewelry, a tube of pink lipstick, and a perfume bottle onto the bench behind her. Jaine donned the teal sheath, fastened on her glittery rhinestone earrings and matching necklace, and then asked Krystal to clasp the accompanying bracelet.

"You look fabulous," Krystal marveled, stepping back after completing her task.

Jaine fluffed her hair around her shoulders, examined herself in the mirror. She'd used the makeup techniques Krystal taught her, including curling her eyelashes and applying lip liner. "Thanks!"

She lifted her cell phone and noticed a voice mail from Shauna. Jaine hoped her sister had left the address of the latest party location.

"I'm meeting friends for a drink, but have a good time." Krystal waved on her way out the door.

Jaine perched on the bench, listening to her message, alone in the dressing room. Shauna's voice rambled, "Jaine, I need help. Can you pick up Amber from Melissa's and let her spend the night? Melissa came down with a fever. You'd have to miss the party, but, well, you've already missed a lot of it. And I have no one else to ask."

Jaine deleted the message and groaned when the phone chirped in her hand. Shauna again. She could ignore the call. But, what if poor Amber was still trapped in a germ-infested house, awaiting a ride? Her muscles tensing, Jaine answered with a reluctant hello.

"There you are!" Shauna exclaimed. "I'm glad I reached you. Didn't you get my message?"

"I just heard it."

"I'm so sorry, Jaine, but would you mind skipping the party? I know you're not into barhopping and I never get a night out. And I feel like I should be here, with Bree being my twin."

Ah, the twin card, the reminder that no matter how hard Jaine tried, she'd never be as chummy with her sisters as they were to one another. The twins had used that excuse a few times over the years, like when Bree won two tickets to a rock concert and offered the second one to Shauna. In Jaine's family, the twins were blood and Jaine was water.

Jaine got up and paced in the deserted locker room. So much for enjoying the party she arranged. Jaine could decline, but if Bree had to choose one sister to attend, she would want her twin. This was Bree's special evening, not hers.

"Okay." Jaine slouched against a locker. "Give me the address."

"Thanks, Jaine! You're a lifesaver. Can you keep her till around three or four o'clock tomorrow? I may be a little hung-over."

"It's my day off, so that's fine."

"Thanks, sis, I owe you one."

That was for damn sure.

After Jaine clocked out in the main office, she strode toward the front entrance. A golf cart coasted in her direction, Dylan at the wheel.

He pressed down on the brake until the cart stopped. "Whoa, bombshell dress. Where are you going all dolled up?"

"I was headed to my sister's bachelorette party, but I got called for overnight babysitting duty instead." Jaine fingered her rhinestone necklace and tried to sound light. "Oh well.

128

I'll have more fun with Amber than clubbing."

"That's nice of you to help out, but it doesn't seem fair you have to miss the party." Dylan frowned slightly.

"It's no big deal. I'd better get going, though, before Amber picks up more germs. Her friend got sick."

Jaine intended to pump sanitizer into her niece's hands the second Amber entered the car. Between the wedding preparations and her job, Jaine couldn't risk being Puke Princess Number 2.

"How about you bring her to the park tomorrow morning?" Dylan rested a hand on the steering wheel. "I'll meet you up front and we can all go on rides together. Give you a behind-the-scenes tour."

Jaine's pulse accelerated, and she pictured squeezing close to Dylan on the train and other attractions. Amber would love spending a day at the theme park. Except. . .what if her niece discovered Jaine's other identity? Although the backup Cinderella had castle duty, Amber might overhear something.

"I don't know. . . ." she hedged.

"A tour would give you authentic details for your future projects. I can tell you the history of the rides." Dylan unfurled a winning grin.

Jaine shifted her duffel bag to her other shoulder. "There's one problem. I didn't tell my family I've been playing Cinderella. I only mentioned the marketing position. My sisters aren't horrible like Cinderella's stepsisters, but they have their moments."

Dylan folded his arms across his chest. "Let me get this straight. The assertive marketing person who talked me into creating a job for her is afraid of her sisters?"

"I didn't feel like hearing their wisecracks. Come on, isn't there anything you've ever kept from your family? Besides your little keg party on the Swan Princess?"

He pondered that for a moment. "I didn't tell them right away when I got a tattoo."

Now it was her turn to elevate an eyebrow. "You have a tattoo? I'm almost afraid to ask. . .where? And what is it?"

"I'll show you tomorrow."

Jaine ought to make up an excuse. Even putting aside her Cinderella secret, hanging out with the boss she had kissed was dicey. Of course, the insider park tidbits could prove useful. And it wasn't as if Dylan had invited her for a private dinner. What was more innocent than a crowded theme park with Amber chaperoning?

"Okay, but I'm warning you, I don't do roller coasters. I'd better go. Amber's waiting."

"Want a lift to your car? That will save you a few minutes."

"Sure." Jaine climbed into the passenger seat beside Dylan. Their knees touched, and a chill jolted through her body.

Dylan flicked the key, shifted into forward, and tapped the gas with his foot. He steered the cart along the gravel path toward the front of the park, veered left, and drove alongside the tall wooden fence enclosing the property. Dylan jumped down to unlock the gate, hopped back onto the cart, and navigated them into the lot.

Someone stood beside Jaine's car, watching the golf cart approach, but she couldn't make out his features. Then she recognized the light blue Chevrolet filling the space beside hers. Sean.

Dylan's chin jutted forward. "You've got company. How was the drive-in, by the way?"

"I fell asleep," Jaine muttered.

"You *fell asleep*? In the car? Are you serious?" He pinned an incredulous gaze on her.

"Yes, my irritating new boss is working me hard, and I fell asleep, okay?"

"Sounds like an exciting date." Dylan chuckled.

"Hush, he's right there."

"Hush? Is that what you'll tell your niece when she tries to stay up past her bedtime?"

"I just say that to annoying golf cart drivers," Jaine retorted.

Dylan pressed on the brake until it locked into place. He parked before her Toyota where he and Sean exchanged nods.

"Thanks for the ride." Jaine stepped down to the pavement.

"Have a good night. Try to stay awake, Jaine." Dylan rocketed ahead with the golf cart and looped back around toward the gate.

Ugh! Now Sean would know she'd told him.

Jaine summoned a smile for Sean. "Hi. What's up?"

He dragged his gaze from the departing golf cart to Jaine. "I wanted to tell you to have fun tonight. You look terrific."

"Thank you. I had an unexpected change in plans though. My sister needs me to babysit, so I'm off to fetch my niece."

"That's too bad. I know how much work you put into the party."

"I'm disappointed, but it will be nice to spend quality time with Amber. We're coming to the park tomorrow so she should have a good day." Jaine fished out her keys, hoping Sean would get the hint.

"You're coming here on your day off?" Sean shook his head and dug his own keys out of his shorts pocket. "There's only so much fairy tale stuff I can take in one week."

He had a point. What sane person wanted to spend extra, unpaid time hanging out at work? If Sean, or even Krystal, had made the offer, Jaine would have passed, but with Dylan as her tour guide, she couldn't resist.

Chapter Twelve

As Jaine approached the main gate with her niece, ten minutes behind schedule, she spotted Dylan scanning the crowd for their arrival. She almost didn't recognize him. In his Mets cap, shades, and T-shirt, he blended in with the tourists.

Dylan stole a surreptitious glance at his watch, and quickening her pace, Jaine ushered Amber to the head of the line. "Sorry we're late. My pancakes burned. We went out for doughnuts."

"Remind me never to eat your cooking. Hey, Amber. I'm Dylan." He extended his hand. With a shy smile, she accepted the handshake.

Jaine clamped her lips together, suppressing her amusement at Amber's bashfulness. Minutes before, her niece had chattered non-stop about her favorite boy band.

Dylan asked the teenage girl in the sales booth to stamp their hands. After she applied the purple 'Sunday' letters, he led Jaine and Amber through the turnstile. "Do you ladies like getting wet?"

"Yes," Amber said, at the precise second Jaine answered, "Sorry, we can't do the water park. We didn't bring bathing suits."

When Amber forgot to ask about the water slides, Jaine didn't suggest swinging by her niece's house to retrieve a suit.

Then she'd have to shadow Amber around the splash pad, dodging ground sprays, spitting dolphins, and the bucket dump. No way did Jaine intend to prance around Dylan in her scoopneck Tankini.

"I'm not talking about the water park," Dylan said. "Lots of people go on the Mermaid Grotto Water Rapids in regular clothes. How do you expect to promote it if you don't know that? Come on, we might make it before there's a line."

"Wait a minute. *You* wait in line?" Jaine asked.

"I eavesdrop and listen to what guests think of the park."

As they followed him through the grounds, Amber announced, "We didn't go on the rapids last time. Aunt Jaine didn't think the weather was warm enough."

"Sounds like your aunt is a wimp," Dylan said.

Jaine rolled her eyes as Amber giggled. So this was how the day would go, with these two ganging up on her. No surprise that even an eight-year-old girl succumbed to Dylan's charisma.

Harold waved from his spot sweeping the sidewalk, and Jaine wondered how many miles he would log on his pedometer today. They passed a teenage boy hefting a water bucket over to one of the many gardens sprinkled throughout the park. Gladiolus, begonias, and cannas bloomed near the carousel, with two gnomes standing guard.

"I never noticed these beautiful flowers." Jaine lingered before the garden. "I guess I'm always focused on getting over to the cast—"

Dylan elbowed her in the side. Oops. She glanced at Amber, but her niece was busy consulting her map. Ten minutes in the park and Jaine had almost blown her cover after her measures to bury any traces of Cinderella. Jaine had

134

pushed her ponytail through the back of a baseball cap and shielded her eyes with sunglasses. She'd allowed herself a hint of lip gloss, so she didn't appear *too* dowdy, but no kids would out her as royalty in front of Amber, that was for sure.

Unless she opened her kingdom-sized mouth.

On the way to the rapids, Dylan greeted a woman in a gray tank top and yoga pants adorned with cherry blossoms. A stretchy Aztec-patterned headband smoothed back her dark strands.

"Hey, Brooke, what number?" Dylan asked.

"Just 342. I was hoping to reach 500 by now, but my sinuses have been killing me this summer. I'm shooting for ten laps today though." Brooke sipped from her water bottle. Her bloodshot eyes screamed of allergies.

"Are you kidding? That's an incredible number. You've still got plenty of time." Dylan raised his hand for a high five. She slapped it, her engagement ring scintillating in the sunlight.

"Thanks, Dylan. Appreciate the support. Have a great day." Nodding at Jaine and Amber, she strolled past them.

"What was that about?" Jaine asked as they continued toward the rapids. Amber scampered ahead of them.

"That was Brooke, our resident thrill seeker," Dylan said. "She's one of our season passholders. Her goal is to ride Wolf Run a thousand times by next July."

"A thousand times!" Jaine cringed at the thought.

"She's a coaster junkie. She's ridden over two hundred across the country. You should see her car. It's covered in coaster decals."

"She looks so mellow. Like a yoga instructor." Jaine followed Dylan into a waiting area for the Mermaid Grotto

Water Rapids.

"Brooke *is* a yoga instructor. Sometimes coaster junkies are the people you'd least expect. You never know, Jaine. Maybe you'll turn into one of them."

"I don't foresee that happening."

Few visitors had reached the rapids ride yet, making their wait less than five minutes. Jaine crammed her hat and glasses into a small cubby near the boarding dock and stepped down after her companions onto a round vessel with six high-backed seats. They clipped safety belts into place and the college-aged ride operator cocked a thumbs-up.

A few seconds later, they were drifting along a lazy river. The raft floated toward a miniature island inhabited by a trio of mermaid statues, long painted green tails perched on rocks.

"See, Jaine, nice and calm," Dylan commented, right before water squirted from a mermaid's mouth and resulted in a dead-on splash to Jaine's nose.

"Yeah, calm," Jaine grumbled.

Her niece and Dylan, both dry, exchanged smirks. A female rider screamed from the vessel ahead of them, not a positive sign of things to come. Their own vessel rounded the U-turn, and a cannon thundered from beneath the surface. To Jaine's extreme satisfaction, a gush of water soaked Dylan's shirt and Amber's long brown mane. Amber squealed in delight.

Whew! Jaine had escaped the cannon with a light spray against her bare legs. Once the ride ended, though, all three were equally saturated. Retrieving her belongings from the cubby, Jaine admitted to herself that the cold water felt refreshing in the eighty-five degree heat.

"That was fun!" Outside the exit gate, Amber fisted the

side of her purple top and squeezed out a river of droplets. "What's next?"

"How about a ride that's truly nice and calm," Jaine suggested, patting her niece with napkins from her purse.

"Told you she was wimpy." Dylan poked Amber in the side.

Jaine shook back the wet ponytail sticking to her neck. "I am not wimpy!"

"You kind of are," Amber said.

Dylan's trickling shirt clung to him, hinting at solid six-pack abs. Jaine stared for a second and he stared back, but not at her face. Oh, man. She must resemble one of those airhead girls who entered wet T-shirt contests at beach bars. Jaine glued her arms across her chest.

Dylan turned to Amber. "Let's do the hay ride and antique cars, and then we'll hit the water chutes when we get hot."

"Okay," she agreed. "And Cinderella's Castle. Don't forget that."

If the girl was old enough to describe boy band members as cute, shouldn't she be too old to sit on Cinderella's lap?

"Don't worry, Cinderella's unforgettable." Dylan winked at Jaine over Amber's head.

After a brief stopover in the restroom where Jaine and Amber toweled off, they re-joined Dylan. He held a cardboard frame bordering a photograph of their rapids adventure. A camera suspended from a tree had captured a shot of them, slick as harbor seals.

Jaine winced. "You bought the cheesy picture?"

"Of course I didn't buy it. My family owns the park."

"I look like a witch hexed me with a bad hair day."

"You look like you were having a great time."

Jaine observed her wide smile and sparkling eyes. Damn. He was right. "You were having a great time, too," she countered, pointing at his grinning mouth.

"I still am." Dylan locked gazes with her and Jaine's heart thundered.

They broke the connection as Amber interrupted, "Come on, let's go on more rides."

"Yes, ma'am," Dylan agreed.

They boarded Tom Thumb's Hay Ride and Rapunzel's Tower Twirl (spinning towers rather than teacups) without a wait, but stood in line for the antique cars.

As the family ahead of them piled into a car, Amber hung over the railing. "We're next. I'll take pink and you guys can have the orange one."

"I thought we were all going together," Jaine said.

Amber huffed out a sigh, a clone of her mother at that age. Jaine allowed herself a dash of smug satisfaction. *Good luck during the teen years, sis.*

Her niece scowled at her. "I'm not a little kid. I can drive by myself. Right, Dylan?"

"I think you can handle it. Tell you what. If you don't crash, I'll take you to get a Storybook Valley driver's license."

"Cool!"

The young female ride operator beckoned Amber forward, and she settled behind the steering wheel of the pink car. She smirked at her aunt, pleased with her triumph.

"Relax, Aunt Jaine." Dylan clapped a hand on Jaine's shoulder as the operator nodded in their direction. "It's not a go-cart. She'll be fine. Besides, we'll be watching her the whole time."

Jaine mimicked her niece's pout. "Okay, but I get to drive."

"I wonder if it's too late for me to hitch a ride with Amber," Dylan muttered, nudging open the gate.

"Very funny." Jaine manned the wheel of the orange car and Dylan squeezed beside her.

At the operator's signal, she stepped on the silver gas pedal and they coasted forward. The winding track led them past miniature replicas of the witch's house from *Hansel and Gretel*, Sleeping Beauty's Castle, and other fairy tale-inspired scenes. They drove beneath the Troll Bridge, and fog billowed around them until they emerged back into the sunlight.

"This ride was my idea, you know," Dylan informed Jaine. "When I was a kid, I told my grandfather that every other amusement park had antique cars, so we needed them, too. We brainstormed the plans for the track on my birthday."

"Wow. I got dolls for my birthday. You got antique cars. My family and I came on this ride when I was a kid. My sisters had their own car, so I rode with my parents."

Her mother had loved day trips, planning outings to apple orchards, vineyards, art exhibitions, an elk farm, music festivals, and even a sky ride chair lift that soared over the mountains. Eventually, the twins grew busy with friends, but Jaine and her parents continued their monthly excursions.

Jaine focused on the upcoming house from Red Riding Hood as the hole in her heart expanded.

"We probably walked right past each other," Dylan said. "I was here all the time. What'd you look like?"

"Pigtails. Glasses since fourth grade."

He chuckled. "That narrows it down to half the girls who have ever visited. Did you go on the train? I used to sit behind my granddad and ride around all day, playing video games."

"I thought boys were gross back then, so I wouldn't have noticed." Jaine waved across the tracks to her smug niece.

"Trust me, you would have noticed. I was damn cute."

I'll bet you were.

"Really? What happened?" Jaine asked.

"You'd better watch that mouth. I can extend your Cinderella reign."

"Not buying it. You need my marketing savvy. Hey, isn't that your father?" Nearing the exit, Jaine removed her foot from the gas pedal and they idled to a stop. She gestured toward the ride operator helping Amber to disembark.

"Yeah. He's not usually here this early." Dylan sounded tense.

Will Callahan motioned to Jaine, and she pressed on the gas. He raised his hand once she had gone far enough. Dylan hopped from the car.

"Why are you and Jaine going on rides?" Will asked. "What's going on?"

Ouch. Jaine flinched at his stern tone.

Dylan's jaw set in a firm line. "I'm giving our marketing coordinator a tour, making sure she's experienced all the attractions."

"I'm babysitting my niece. So today was a good day for Dylan to show me around. That's her ahead of us." Jaine dipped her head toward the exit gate.

Grunting, Will aimed a suspicious look at his son.

"We'd better catch up to her. We have more to do." Without another word, Dylan brushed past his father.

"Have a nice day, Mr. Callahan." Jaine hurried to join Dylan. Amber had dashed into the station that hawked Storybook Valley driver's licenses.

Dylan tugged on the brim of his baseball cap. "Sorry about the inquisition. Told you, I have a reputation."

"Soon he'll appreciate what a great job you're doing. He'll realize you're not that irresponsible kid anymore." Jaine lightened the mood with a little teasing. "He'll see you're not the same playboy, lady killer, planner of keg parties—"

"Got it," Dylan interrupted, giving her a playful shove. "Let's go."

Ten minutes later, much to Jaine's dismay, they were strolling toward Cinderella's Castle. Amber strummed the new license hanging from a lanyard around her neck. Her bright smile mirrored the one in her driver's license photograph.

"Isn't this cool, Aunt Jaine? Doesn't it look real?"

Sure, if the DMV issued licenses that read "approved by Prince Charming" and dangled from fluorescent orange cords.

"Yeah, it does." Jaine exchanged amused glances with Dylan.

They trudged up the hill toward Cinderella's Castle. Amber meandered ahead, sipping from a juice box.

"Wouldn't want to make this hike every day." Dylan swabbed sweat off his brow and tossed her a grin. "Would you, Jaine?"

Jaine glared at him. "No, but at least I'm wearing sneakers. Your poor Cinderella has to slog around in glass slippers. I hope you treat her well."

"I gave her fresh squeezed lemonade once."

"You should do that more often."

"How chivalrous of you to worry about our Cinderella."

She smothered a laugh. They lagged behind Amber

through the archway into the castle. A little girl buried her head in her mother's side while her family tried coaxing her toward Cinderella.

"But, Hailey, you love princesses." Her father held up the camera. "Don't you want a picture for your photo album?"

The girl chewed the edge of her dark braid, shaking her head. Jaine's backup Cinderella abandoned her throne and approached the family. Jaine hoped she wasn't gawking, but boy, was it odd to see someone else inhabiting the ball gown. Dylan's cousin Wendy looked about Jaine's age with striking blue eyes under the fringe of golden Gibson Girl bangs. Soft pink blush tinged her cheeks with subtle rosiness.

Wendy knelt before the little girl. "Hailey, I love your purple sneakers. Did I see them light up?"

Clinging to her mother, Hailey gave a quick nod.

"Would you like to hear my favorite color? It's purple. Do you want to know why?" As Hailey's shoulders lifted, Wendy continued, "Purple is a royal color. Could you stand beside me so I can get a better view of those beautiful shoes?"

Hailey let go of her mother and shuffled over to the princess. Interesting, Wendy's strategy worked. The other day, Jaine failed in the same situation, disappointing the parents.

"Look, your shoes are lighting up again." Wendy clapped her slender hands. "Those are the most magnificent shoes in the entire kingdom."

Damn, she was good. Jaine tore her gaze from the scene. She'd lost track of her niece, but after a few seconds located Amber peering at the glass slipper display case.

"I don't know who was more fascinated to see Cinderella, you or that little girl," Dylan murmured in Jaine's ear.

She inhaled the scent of his cologne and forced words out of her dry mouth. "I'm jealous. She's so smooth. Too bad *she* can't be your main Cinderella."

"Wendy has played Cinderella for years, but now she's busy helping her parents run the Storybook Valley Inn and Grill. Don't worry. You're smooth, too. Didn't you see the way Noah reacted? You won him over just like you win everyone over."

"You think I win people over?" Jaine's envy had long since disappeared, replaced by a more confusing emotion. With his baseball cap, collared polo shirt, and shorts, Dylan could have been any husband wandering the park with a wife and kid.

"My grandfather loved you. You should have heard him raving about how terrific you are. Rory and Tiara said nice things, too. And look how you talked me into offering you a job that didn't exist. You're a natural charmer. Didn't you know that?"

"I guess I didn't. Thanks."

As Amber posed with Cinderella's arm around her shoulders, Jaine snapped a picture with her phone. At her niece's insistence, she sent the photo to Shauna. Not surprisingly, Jaine's sister didn't respond. Perhaps she was in the shower, away from her cell, but more likely, she had conked out in bed, trusting that Jaine would tend to problems.

Had Bree and the bridesmaids gotten trashed last night? Their brunch reservations probably went unused. She should have left bottles of Gatorade in the fridge to quell hangovers.

Amber wanted to visit the medieval playground and Jaine agreed, relieved for a break. Her niece scrambled across the turreted bridge and explored tunnels leading to curvy slides and majestic towers. Swings creaking, parents pushed their children up toward the cloudless blue sky.

Jaine drank from a Storybook Valley water bottle as she and Dylan relaxed on a shaded bench. Therese gave her the bottle on her first day and she noticed that every ride operator carried an identical version, along with sunscreen. That reminded Jaine, she ought to reapply sunscreen on herself and Amber.

"So how come you got off so easily?" Jaine asked Dylan. "Tiara mentioned the fairy tale names in your family. Why don't you have one?"

"You mean she didn't tell you?"

"Wait a minute, you do have one?"

"Promise you won't laugh?" Dylan leaned against the slats of the bench.

"Hell, no, but tell me anyway."

"My first name was after my mother's brother, Dylan, but my middle name is Peter."

"Peter?" Jaine considered that for a moment. Seemed ordinary enough. Unless. . . . "As in Peter Pan?" A giggle rose in her throat and she sputtered out a mouthful of water.

"It's not that funny."

"I beg to differ. Have you had any recent run-ins with Captain Hook? Where are the Lost Boys?"

"How would you like me to throw you to the crocodiles?" Dylan lightly kicked her ankle. "You know what's not funny though? They still think of me as Peter Pan. The boy who won't grow up."

Sobering, Jaine groped in her canvas bag for her bottle of lotion. "But there's a big difference between you and Peter. He wants to stay in Neverland. You don't."

They sat in silence for a moment. Jaine squirted a white

144

dollop into her palm, greased it onto her arms. "Hey, you promised to show me your tattoo." She slathered sunscreen over her legs.

Dylan peeled back his sleeve, revealing the skin around his shoulder and upper back. Jaine moved closer, resisting an overpowering urge to touch the black and red lines. She couldn't see the whole tattoo since the design traveled down his back, but she distinguished a coiled, scaled dragon and bursts of flames.

"Whoa, this is no cheerful Dazzle the Dragon," Jaine said. "You chose Dazzle's exact opposite, didn't you? Was that an act of rebellion?"

He released his sleeve, and she brushed off a pang of disappointment as the dragon disappeared. Until this moment, Jaine hadn't realized she fancied tattoos on men.

"That might have been my first reason, but I liked what dragons represent. Freedom. Power. Strength. Wisdom. Courage."

All that from a tattoo? Now Jaine really yearned to inspect it close up. "How come you didn't get it on your arm?"

"Storybook Valley doesn't allow visible tattoos on employees. If I ever had to help out, covering it would be a hassle."

"A logical rebel. Interesting." Jaine spurted a couple more dabs of lotion and applied it to her face.

"My family has called me a hell raiser, wild child, and playboy, but no one has ever called me a logical rebel." Dylan wiped the top of her nose with his fingertip. "You had a dot of sunscreen there."

"You could use some yourself."

"I hate touching that gunk. How about you do it for me?"

Fighting a tremble in her hands, Jaine spread lotion across

his cheeks and chin. His whiskers felt rough and despite the cool cream, she drew back for a few seconds as if his face were ablaze. Heat radiated between them and she didn't think it emanated from the sun.

"You won't leave me looking like a clown, will you?" Dylan asked more softly than usual.

"It's tempting, I must admit." Jaine needed to maintain their trademark banter even though she ached to trace along his rugged jaw line until she reached the curve of his lips.

As she worked on his neck, Jaine swore that his breathing accelerated. An ache clenched Jaine's chest. She yearned to kiss him, but they couldn't cross that line. Not again.

Jaine swiftly rubbed in the remaining sunscreen and then extended the bottle. No way was she rubbing it on the rest of his body. "There, the clown stripes are gone."

"Thanks. Sorry about the scruffiness." Their fingers met around the bottle and Jaine lowered her arm.

"Yeah, you and your razor need to spend quality time to-gether." Jaine didn't mention she was a sucker for a guy with stubble. And tattoos, apparently. Who knew?

Amber skipped over from the playground. "This is the best day ever! Dylan, are you coming to my aunt's wedding?"

"Your aunt's wedding?"

"Yeah. With Aunt Jaine. You're her boyfriend, right?"

Jaine gasped. No! Amber had not just asked Dylan if he was her boyfriend. This wasn't happening.

She swatted her niece in the arm, harder than necessary. "He's not my boyfriend, Amber! He's my boss! Of course he isn't coming to the wedding."

"Oh. Okay." Amber peered into the depths of Jaine's bag. "Can I have another juice box, Aunt Jaine? And can we have lunch?"

Jaine popped a straw into a green apple juice box and thrust the drink at her niece. "In a few minutes. We'll redo your sunscreen when we get there."

She braved a sideways look at Dylan. He displayed a lop-sided grin that stole her breath away.

"Kids," Jaine murmured. "They think they know everything."

His grin faded, and he regarded Jaine with a concentration that set her pulse hammering again. "Are you taking Sean to the wedding?"

"I haven't thought about it yet." She'd had enough of discussing her love life, or more aptly, her lack of love life, with the guy who was off-limits. "Who wants a hamburger?"

Chapter Thirteen

From: Dylan Callahan
Subject: Coaster Junkies
Date: Tuesday, August 4 06:45 P.M.
To: Jaine Andersen

Hi Jaine,
Had fun with you and Amber. Next time, I'm getting you onto that rollercoaster, though. I'll turn you into a coaster junkie yet.
Dylan

From: Jaine Andersen
Subject: When Cows Jump Over the Moon
Date: Tuesday, August 4 07:00 P.M.
To: Dylan Callahan

Amber and I had fun, too. I even liked the rapids. P.S. - NO WAY am I going on the rollercoaster. Wasn't it enough I did the water chute?
Jaine

Jaine curled up on the couch and watched a sitcom rerun, missing half the jokes. Her gaze kept wandering toward the tablet on her coffee table. When her in-box chimed, she lunged for the device. Jaine grinned at the second message from Dylan.

From: Dylan Callahan
Subject: RE: When Cows Jump Over the Moon
Date: Tuesday, August 4 07:15 P.M.
To: Jaine Andersen
The water chute just has one hill! Come on, don't you want Amber to think you're cool?
D

Jaine hit reply and tapped into the message box.

From: Jaine Andersen
Subject: Cool Quotient
Date: Tuesday, August 4 07:17 P.M.
To: Dylan Callahan

For your information, Amber thought I was very cool for going on the water chute! Besides, if I'd gone on the roller-coaster with you guys, who would've taken the pictures?
Your Cool Marketing Coordinator

Jaine concentrated on the TV though she aimed longing

glances at the tablet. She jumped at a couple false alarms (an email from her father and a group bridesmaid memo from Bree), but finally Dylan responded.

From: Dylan Callahan
Subject: A Better Idea
Date: Tuesday, August 4 07:30 p.m.
To: Jaine Andersen

You were mildly cool for going on the water chute. Speaking of pictures, how about one of Cinderella riding the roller-coaster? Can't you see that on our next brochure? So cool. . . .

D

From: Jaine Andersen
Subject: Wendy
Date: Tuesday, August 4 07:35 P.M.
To: Dylan Callahan

What a great idea! Do you want to tell your cousin Wendy or should I?

From: Dylan Callahan
Subject: Sarcastic Princess
Date: Tuesday, August 4 07:45 P.M.
To: Jaine Andersen
Ha ha. I don't remember the real Cinderella being this smart alecky.

From: Jaine Andersen
Subject: Too Much Time in Fairy Tale Land
Date: Tuesday, August 4 07:50 P.M.
To: Dylan Callahan

The "real" Cinderella?????????

Jaine staked out her email for the rest of the night, but Dylan didn't write back. She was addicted to their exchanges. Sending to each other's private email accounts rather than through inter-office email made it even more personal.

What was he doing? Watching TV? Walking the dog? With a sigh, she shut down the tablet at 10 p.m.

As Jaine climbed into bed, she glimpsed the cardboard-framed picture on the oak bureau of her, Dylan, and Amber in the water rapids vessel. Jaine clicked off her lamp.

She stared at the ceiling for an hour before surrendering to a restless sleep.

***

The next afternoon, Jaine read a picture book about Thumbelina during story time. She displayed each illustration to the circle of cross-legged children before flipping the page. Dylan appeared as she was closing the castle for her lunch break.

"I brought lunch. But, I've got dibs on half." Dylan held a paper plate of fried dough laced with confectionary sugar. The huge golden brown oval fanned out to the plate's edges.

151

In his other hand, he carried a plastic cup brimming with lemonade.

"Ooh, yum. Your grandmother would freak out, though, if she saw me with powdered sugar in this dress." Jaine shut the door, paranoid that Lois Callahan was lurking outside in one of the pumpkin coaches.

Dylan displayed a pile of napkins, half-tucked beneath the plate. "Logical rebel, remember?"

"Hang on." Jaine pried off her glass slippers and fetched fluorescent green flip flops out of her zip-up travel bag. She eased her feet into the rubber foot beds and dropped onto a plush bench. "So much better. A little tip from your sister. Keep my secret?"

"Totally. Just don't forget to switch shoes. That's all I need, a Cinderella in beach gear." Dylan joined her on the bench and positioned the plate between them.

"Beach Bum Cinderella. Hmm, how can I make that worthy of inclusion in the Cinderella Curse?" Jaine touched a finger to her lip, pretending to think. "We could lay out towels for story time. There's some around town with Harley Davidson logos and the Corona label. I'll drink a Pina Colada on the throne and read the story through goggles."

"You could read *Puff, The Magic Dragon* and tell them about the alleged drug references." Dylan extended her lemonade. "As long as we're brainstorming."

"Good idea! And throw a beach ball at the kids to make sure they're paying attention. Forget the throne. I can sit on one of those huge inflatable pool floats. Like a giant swan! What do you think?"

Dylan dragged a hand through his hair. The column of his throat muscles traveled up and down. "I think you're amazing. You're creative, and funny, and keep me on my toes. I've never met anyone like you. I wish I could get you out of my mind, but I can't."

Shock, then a jolt of heat, flooded through Jaine's body. The castle seemed smaller and energy pulsed between them, stirring hairs on the back of her arms and along the nape of her neck. She couldn't formulate a response, had no clue what the correct response was. Jaine knew how she wanted to answer. . .but that would change everything.

"If I make you uncomfortable, just shut me up," Dylan went on. "We said we'd forget that kiss, but every time I see you around Sean, it drives me crazy. I'm afraid that if I don't make a move, either he'll scoop you up or some other guy will."

"What. . .what are you saying?" Jaine curled her fingers around her cup.

"That depends. If you don't want to talk about this, then I'll stop. I won't ever bring it up again because I'll never harass you, Jaine. I want you to feel safe working here." Dylan's eyes fixed on Jaine's. When she didn't speak he continued, "I need to ask you something. Am I the only one feeling this way?"

Here was her chance to play it safe. To keep things professional. But his gaze mesmerized her and Jaine had no desire to break the spell.

"No," she murmured. "You're not the only one."

Dylan's lips pressed down on hers, igniting the most exhilarating kiss Jaine had ever experienced. She returned it with an ardor that stunned her. The plate of fried dough toppled to the faux marble floor and Jaine regained her senses. She drew away from the crisp woodsy fragrance of his cologne.

"What now?" she asked.

"Will you go on a date with me?"

"That depends. Are you taking me to the drive-in, or do I get the grand gesture of the horseback riding and picnic?"

"The grand gesture." He offered the crooked grin that made her pulse speed up. "Unless it rains. Then you get bowling."

"Deal." Jaine loved how at ease she felt around him even though her heart thumped double-time inside her rib cage.

He hesitated. "I want to say something. If things don't work out, I promise it won't affect your job."

"I appreciate that, Dylan, and I trust you. I'm more worried about your parents. They're already skeptical of me. I don't want them thinking I'm just another one of your airheads." Oops. She should have put that more tactfully. There were drawbacks to feeling she could tell him anything. "Um, no offense?"

"It's okay. You're right." Dylan scrubbed a hand over his face. "I'd prefer to keep it quiet, too. That way we can see where this goes without everyone's attention on us. And to be honest, I got myself into a mess last year."

"What happened?"

Dylan got up and brushed a napkin over the confectionary sugar path dusting the floor. "Let's save that story for after I've impressed you."

Chapter Fourteen

Clasping her hand, Dylan led Jaine through a sunlit rolling meadow overlooking the Hudson River and the blue green peaks of the Catskills. He walked past families occupying rustic cedar pavilions and steered her down a secluded trail.

Jaine dodged a hanging branch as they trekked along the rocky path, grass and pine needles crunching underfoot. She had hoped for the promised picnic, but they were hiking first, which didn't thrill her rumbling stomach.

"I get it," Jaine panted, following the curving trail. "You're keeping me busy because of my history of falling asleep on dates."

"Hiking is good exercise. It's about time you saw some of these trails you've lived near your whole life."

"I've seen them. . .in magazines."

Dylan guided her around one more bend and then halted in a clearing. Jaine surveyed the fleece blanket spread across the ground and the handwoven wicker basket in the center. He wasn't dragging her on a hike after all. Dylan had chosen the perfect spot.

"Dylan! This is fabulous." Jaine strolled toward the blanket, tugging Dylan's arm behind her.

She released his hand, knelt, and opened the basket. Compartments on the inside lid secured gleaming silverware and ivory china. Jaine gaped at the feast that stuffed the basket: assorted crispy breads wrapped in parchment paper, savory biscuits and homemade preserves, cold meats and cheeses, a container of Greek style pasta salad, plump green grapes, fruit skewers, and more. Dylan crouched beside her on the plush blanket and withdrew a bouquet of six red roses from the basket. She hadn't even noticed the flowers, too distracted by the smorgasbord, but now Jaine drank in their splendor. Dylan extended the bouquet, and she inhaled the fragrance.

"Dylan Callahan, I had no idea you were such a romantic!" Jaine kissed his cheek, hoping he didn't notice the tears prickling in her eyes.

No one had ever gone to this much trouble for her. She was always the one planning special things for others. Bree's bridal shower and bachelorette party. Amber's last couple birthdays. She'd even helped a college friend organize her parents' surprise anniversary party. "How on earth did you do this?"

"Will it shatter the mood if I admit I hired a catering company?"

"No, it's a relief because if this was an example of your cooking, then you'd be horrified when you saw my freezer. It's filled with Stouffer's and Tyson." Jaine sniffed the roses once more and lowered the bouquet to the blanket. She slipped out the dishes, cutlery, and linen napkins and prepared place settings for each of them. "Did they deliver, too?"

"That's part of the service. I read about it in the newspaper and thought it would be a neat idea if there was a girl I wanted to impress." He nudged her shoulder.

Jaine's cheeks warmed. To distract herself, she inspected rich frosted brownies in wax bags and a tin of gold-foiled chocolate truffles. "It worked. And I'm the only one you've tried it on?"

"You're a princess. I had to give you the royal treatment." Dylan sprawled on his side, extending his blue-jeaned legs and boots. Jaine had worn jeans and leather boots also, for their sunset horseback ride. She'd selected her cutest skinny jeans, with sparkles on the pockets.

After they filled their plates, Jaine ventured, "Tell me about the situation you got yourself into. Let me guess. It's over a girl." She sat cross-legged with the dish in her lap.

"When I worked at the ski resort, I made a big mistake. I dated a co-worker. It wasn't anything serious. We were just having fun. At least that's what I thought." The grim twist of Dylan's mouth told Jaine where this story was headed.

"After we went out a few times, she got possessive, so I let her down gently. She retaliated by claiming to management that I was sexually harassing her." He paused and watched a squirrel hopping from branch-to-branch in the distance. A bird trilled in the quiet. "I got fired."

Even though she had expected the revelation, Jaine cringed. "Oh, Dylan. I'm sorry."

"I could have fought her claims, but it wasn't worth it. My dad was retiring, and like I told you before, I'd had enough of working for someone else. This was the trigger I needed."

"That's great your parents supported you after all that happened."

Dylan gulped a long swig of champagne. "Believe me, it wasn't easy to convince them I deserved a chance at taking over the park. If my grandparents and Rory hadn't raised a fuss, they never would have considered the idea. My parents knew I wouldn't harass anyone, but they thought I was an idiot for getting myself into that position. And it's true. I was an idiot, I admit it."

"Maybe, but that girl was obnoxious." Jaine set her plate on the blanket and scooted closer to him.

"Yeah, she was. I never intended to date anyone from work again after the way I got burned." His voice softened. "Then you came along and here we are."

This romance might backfire on both of them big-time, but if Dylan was willing to risk it, so was Jaine. "Whatever happens between us, you can trust me. I'd never make false accusations. I'd never lie how. . .what was the girl's name?"

He fidgeted. "Tawny."

Jaine bit down on her lip before a chuckle flew out. "Oh God, Dylan, that sounds like a stripper."

"I'm well aware of that, thank you."

She sobered, imagining the girl-with-a-stripper-name who had hijacked Dylan's common sense. "I'll bet she looked like one, too, huh?"

"You're a lot more beautiful than she was, Jaine. Inside and out." Squeezing her hand, Dylan raised himself into a seated position. He cupped the sides of Jaine's face, then swooped in and kissed her. He tasted like champagne and strawberries, even yummier than the meal before her.

"Got that?" he murmured, their lips inches apart.

"Got it. Now shut up." With confidence befitting a princess, Jaine once again melded her mouth with his.

* * *

Thursday night, Jaine hung her used Cinderella gown on the to-clean rack in the wardrobe department, a dreamy smile hovering on her lips. She couldn't stop thinking about Dylan. His romantic picnic and the sunset, group horseback ride through clearings and forest. Their good night kiss outside her building.

All the phone calls and texts during the week. Most nights they talked for a couple hours, topics ranging from music and TV shows, to their childhoods, friendships, and embarrassing moments. She'd been considering inviting him to Bree's wedding. He would miss the ceremony due to the Back-to-School Ball, but he could make it for the reception.

Maybe I'll ask him tonight.

Krystal rifled through garments on the rack, cross-checking the day's costume log, and Jaine stepped aside. Her stomach flipping, she plucked her keys out of her purse. A couple more hours until their second date.

"You seem happy," Krystal noted, sending Jaine a sideways glance.

Better tone down the excitement. Jaine busied herself with sliding on her prescription sunglasses. "Do I? Well, my sister is getting married next weekend and the Back-to-School Ball is coming up, too. I'm just in a good mood."

"Uh, huh." Krystal pressed her clipboard against her Red Riding Hood blouse and regarded Jaine, unconvinced. "You were humming."

"No, I wasn't."

"Yeah, you were."

Jaine shuffled through her purse, pretending to hunt for something. She made a show of opening a container of orange Tic Tacs. "Want some?"

"Come on, Jaine. Admit it. You're in love."

Jaine almost choked on a Tic Tac. Why did they make

these things so damn tiny? "Krystal, I'm looking forward to Chinese take-out and watching a movie. Really. That's why I'm happy."

No way would she admit Dylan was picking up Chinese food on his way to her apartment, or that she wanted to rush home and get ready. Plus Jaine needed to call a reporter named Erin who had a question about the Back-to-School Ball. She'd left a few messages on newsroom voice mails, requesting a photographer, and finally someone called her back. She had to get out of here.

Krystal's stare would intimidate the Big Bad Wolf. "Come on, I know that lovesick look. You've fallen for Sean, right? He's such a sweetheart and so cute, too."

Sean. Jaine needed to let him down easy. He had emailed her about another date, and she had procrastinated on a response. She inched closer to the door. "No, you're imagining things."

As her phone chimed, Jaine snatched it from her purse, grateful for the interruption. She studied the text from Dylan.

Come by my office before you leave. Problem.

That didn't sound good. Work-related or date-related?

On my way, Jaine texted back. "I've got to go. Have a good night, Krystal."

Jaine hastened toward the employee cottages, clocked out, and stepped into Dylan's office. His mother occupied a chair across from his desk, a pile of newspapers in her lap.

Dylan rubbed his brow, as if warding off a headache, and gestured toward the other chair. "Take a seat, Jaine."

Jaine's stomach clenched. Whenever they passed each other in the park, even if they didn't talk, Dylan grinned her way. But now he gave off a different vibe. A tense one. She lowered herself into the chair and grasped the armrests. "What's wrong?"

"Thanks to your carelessness, fifty families signed up for the Back-to-School Ball on the wrong date." Therese waved a printout of a spreadsheet and slapped it on the desk.

"Mom, it was a mistake, not carelessness," Dylan said.

"Carelessness leads to mistakes, Dylan. We need to contact these people and offer refunds. Unfortunately, we're going to look incompetent. Nothing like this has ever happened at Storybook Valley."

"How is this possible?" Jaine met Dylan's gaze, implored him to take her side.

"Multiple newspapers published the press release with the wrong date. The flyers were wrong, too." Dylan scraped a hand through his wavy hair. "We screwed up."

Now she understood why Dylan appeared in need of ibuprofen. We. At least he'd said we.

Jaine shook her head, adrenaline spiking through her. "I double-checked the date and time before I sent it to the list of contacts your grandfather gave me. And you approved everything, too. This doesn't make sense, Dylan."

"It's right there in black and white. We overlooked a typo."

Theresa thrust the pile of newspapers onto Jaine's knees. Swallowing, Jaine read the first one, open to the calendar section. Someone had marked a paragraph with a glaring red circle. *The ball will be held August 29*.

A fluttery queasiness spread throughout Jaine's insides. How could it say August twenty-ninth instead of August twenty-second?

"Okay, they must have retyped it for some reason and made a mistake." Jaine rustled to the next paper with a red circle. And the next.

"They're the same, Jaine. The papers couldn't have all made typos." Dylan pushed the yellow flyer across the desk. "Besides, it's on these, too."

Jaine swiped it away from him so hard that the edges crinkled. August twenty-ninth. Damn it. She leaped up and paced the room on unsteady legs. "I don't understand. I double-checked the press release. And the flyers."

"Jaine, you didn't," Therese said sharply. "If you had done an adequate job proofreading, we wouldn't have this problem. Anyway, didn't you notice that the date was wrong on the flyer? They're all over the park."

"I don't know what to say. I was certain everything was correct. And no, I guess I didn't read the flyers again once they were distributed." Jaine watched Dylan shuffle one of the many papers strewn across his desk.

Last night, they had talked on the phone past midnight. He teased her about the chick flicks she rented for their upcoming date. Now all traces of the playful Dylan had disappeared. He'd strived so hard to impress his parents as general manager and her stupid Back-to-School Ball idea had screwed up everything.

"Look at this mess, Dylan. How do you find anything?" Therese appraised the clutter on her son's workspace. "Honestly, I'm not even surprised that this happened."

Jaine gritted her teeth. Would Therese ever appreciate her son's talents and drive? Not with this strike against him. "On second thought, maybe Dylan didn't approve those files. Now I'm wondering if I forgot to send them. It's my fault."

"You sent them." Dylan hurled her a warning look.

"No, I didn't. You reviewed old drafts. I made revisions

and must have gotten confused and changed the date to the one I originally pitched. You didn't get a copy of the new versions. I'm sure of it now."

His arms crossed over his chest. "Yes, I did. We're both at fault."

Jaine wished Therese would leave so she could tell Dylan what a stubborn moron he was and then kiss him hard. His loyalty soothed her frayed nerves like balm.

Gabrielle cleared her throat from the doorway. Without waiting for an invitation, she strutted deeper into the room. "How cute, you're trying to protect each other. Don't you think, though, that if you flirted less, you could focus more on your jobs and avoid these sticky situations?"

Jaine faced her former classmate, a knot coiling in her belly. Gabrielle stood over them, stylish in her single button jacket, silk shell, and pencil skirt.

Therese swiveled her gaze from Gabrielle to her son. "Dylan, what does she mean?"

"I have no idea." Dylan's voice had an edge.

"Oh, come on, Dyl." Gabrielle smirked. "I saw Jaine slathering sunscreen on you and everyone noticed how cozy you two were on the rides. I was running errands around the park, but you guys were so into each other, you didn't even notice me."

Jaine's mouth turned to cotton. "My eight-year-old niece was with us. Dylan was showing us around."

Her pearl bracelet gleaming, Gabrielle waved a dismissive hand. "Harold thinks you're having a fling. I mentioned how chummy you guys were and he loved sharing a little gossip. Something about a kiss by the pond?"

"All right, that's enough. You don't know what the hell

you're talking about." Dylan shoved back his chair and vaulted to his feet.

"For heaven's sake, Dylan!" his mother burst out. "Are you seventeen or twenty-seven? There are plenty of other women to date besides the help."

The help. Jaine's toes curled up inside her shoes. A deep flush edged across her cheeks.

"Gabrielle, what are you doing here? This isn't your business." His jaw clamped tight, Dylan closed the space between him and Gabrielle.

"It's my business if *my* support staff has to waste time calling people and issuing refunds."

"*Your* support staff doesn't have to get involved. I'll handle it." Jaine rose and whipped the spreadsheet off the desk.

"You don't have access to the credit card information, Jaine, so how do you expect to give a refund?"

What were they, back in high school? Could Gabrielle sound any bitchier? Jaine pretended she was dealing with Breezilla and gathered all her mental restraint to keep from snapping.

"I'll reschedule everyone I can and list people who want their money back. That will at least get things started." Before Gabrielle barked a veto, Jaine stalked out of Dylan's office.

Once she sat down at her desk, Jaine gripped her weak knees. She had created a PR nightmare. Every event coordinator feared disasters of this scope. Jaine cupped the mouse, ready to search her emails and Word files to view the mistake for herself. Then she released it and picked up the telephone instead. She would deal with the why and how later. For now, Jaine had a crummy job to tackle.

She swallowed a few times to ease the thickening in her

throat, pushed her shoulders back, and pressed her first phone number.

An hour and a half later, Jaine rapped on Dylan's open door. Everyone else had left for the evening, including Therese, who didn't acknowledge Jaine on the way out.

Dylan glanced up from his computer, expression weary. "How's it going?"

"I reached thirty-nine of the families. Twenty-four switched the date and fifteen requested refunds. I'll follow up with the others tomorrow. Only one person yelled at me. The rest were nice." Jaine held still, her spine erect.

"Thanks. I called the newspapers and asked for a correction. I have a kid collecting flyers from around the park. Why don't you come in early tomorrow and fix it in the computer. I'll have someone distribute new copies."

"Dylan, I still don't understand how this happened. I swear the date was correct. We both checked it." Jaine's voice wobbled, her suppressed emotions brimming to the surface. She wouldn't receive gold stars for her work performance anytime soon.

"I hate to admit Gabrielle is right. . .but she has a point." Dylan leaned back in his chair, arms falling at his sides.

Dullness spread through Jaine's chest at his pained expression. "What do you mean?"

"This mistake shouldn't have happened. Maybe we *were* distracted. Jaine, it kills me to say this, but I think we need to keep our relationship professional."

Jaine clasped her hands together. He was breaking up with her. No more romantic dinners and long phone chats. No more kisses and private jokes. After everything that had happened tonight, she should have expected this, but Jaine hadn't allowed herself to dwell on the possibility. She had focused on calling families, trying to make things right, and in the back of her mind she counted on Dylan to console her. To be there for her.

"I can't lose this job. That will prove my family's right about me, that I *am* a screw-up. And if I fail, I don't want to bring you down with me. You've got to concentrate on your career so that your marketing skills impress everyone else the way they impressed me." Dylan came around the desk and closed his fingers around hers. "I'm sorry, Jaine. This is my fault, not yours. I shouldn't have asked out one of my employees."

Jaine stared at their intertwined fingers and then up into Dylan's taut face. She understood. She did. But that didn't mean she agreed with Dylan, Therese, and Gabrielle assuming she was a lovesick underling daydreaming at her computer and making foolish errors. Yes, he occupied her mind, but it hadn't affected her job performance.

"I get it, Dylan, and it's fine. But if I made a typo, it wasn't because of our relationship. I'm distracted from planning a wedding, running my sisters' errands, and playing Cinderella. My mistake was overextending myself. Trust me, that typo had nothing to do with pining over you." She retracted her hand.

"Jaine, that's not what I meant."

"Look, no hard feelings. Tomorrow we'll be employer/employee again. I'll do my best to make this park—and you—look good. I'll work 110 percent like I do for everything and everyone. But tonight, just let me stew about this crappy day."

"Jaine—"

She strode out his office door and gathered her belongings from her desk.

She'd been naive to hope for a fairy tale ending. No matter how many times Jaine dressed up in a ball gown and donned glass slippers, she wasn't Cinderella the princess.

I'm Cinderella the scullery maid, who no one appreciates.

Chapter Fifteen

Jaine spent an exhausting Friday correcting the flyer fiasco, entertaining children, and making follow-up calls to guests on her lunch break. As she huddled before a mirror beside Krystal, freshening her makeup for the second-to-last Meet and Greet Fireworks Gala of the season, her phone signaled an incoming call. Shauna.

Great. Jaine had dodged a string of texts from Bree, something about drunken wedding guests, along with a note from Shauna begging for help to calm her twin. Sighing, Jaine capped her lipstick and inserted it back into her cosmetics bag. May as well get in the bridal loop. If she didn't respond, her sisters would stalk her.

"What's going on?" Jaine asked. "Bree's in a snit over drunken guests?"

"Campbell's parents decided they want to pay for an open bar at the reception and Bree freaked out," Shauna said. "She thinks his old fraternity brothers will get trashed."

"They're having wine with dinner, right? Can't she ask his family to limit the open bar to the cocktail hour?"

"Campbell wants it for the whole shebang. I told her they should find a way to compromise, but they're not talking to each other. I'm surprised he hasn't caved. Campbell usually gives her whatever she wants."

Jaine forced her feet into the wretched glass slippers. She examined her reflection in the mirror. Gibson Girl wig, tiara, puffy gown. If Shauna could see her now, her chortling would rupture Jaine's eardrum. She shifted her attention back to her conversation.

"Bree's probably acting so bossy that the poor guy's at his breaking point. I'll bet if she was polite, he'd hear her out."

"Can you call her? Maybe if we give her the same advice, she'll listen. She's complaining you're blowing her off."

"I've been busy working! I'll send her a text."

"If I hang up, you can make a quick call," Shauna insisted. "I mean, if you're talking to me, you can talk to her. If that doesn't work, you could convince Campbell to give up the open bar."

"Shauna, I'm swamped! You're lucky I answered my phone."

"Jaine, come on. At least call her when you get home. You come home to your cat and no responsibilities besides cleaning the litter box. I have a kid and I'm tired. Can't you just handle this?"

Jaine leaped from her chair and its legs screeched on the floor. "Are you kidding me? I do your babysitting, grocery shopping, daycare research, and car-pooling. I've planned Bree's bridal shower, bachelorette party, and coordinated tons of wedding details, and you think my only responsibility is taking care of my cat!"

She glimpsed herself in the mirror, red-faced, glossy lips flattened, and nostrils flared. If Jaine listened to Shauna another minute, she'd storm outside and launch a Road Rage attack on the Fairy Tale Express. Kooky Cinderella. One more legend for the Cinderella Curse.

"Goodbye, Shauna." Jaine disconnected and flung down her phone. She ought to hang up on her sisters more often.

"Um, Jaine? You okay?" Krystal rose from the chair beside her, in Red Riding Hood garb. "Are you sure you can handle the Meet and Greet?"

Jaine inhaled and exhaled a few times, adrenaline hurtling through her body. "We've still got five minutes. I'll be okay. I'm just losing patience with my sisters."

"Sounds like you've had a tough week. Therese mentioned the reservation problem."

Jaine shot a look at her. Had she also heard about her involvement with Dylan? Krystal's wholesome Red Riding Hood face showed nothing.

"It's been a long couple days," she conceded.

"Let's meet at your place after the dinner. I'll bring the alcohol." Without waiting for an answer, Krystal tossed back her cape, grasped the handle of her picnic basket, and skipped out the front door.

Jaine had officially stumbled into the Storybook Twilight Zone.

* * *

Several hours later, Jaine related the whole story at her kitchen table while she and Krystal drank Fuzzy Navels and shared chocolate chunk cookies from the supermarket bakery. She filled in her friend on her romance with Dylan, Gabrielle's butting in, and Therese's disgust.

"You mean Dylan's the guy who got you all lovesick? Oh, Jaine. I love him like a brother, but you want someone who will settle down. Dylan's the king of flings." Krystal

crunched another cookie. A fluorescent pink T-shirt embla-
zoned with a butterfly topped her black leggings.

Jaine sipped from her highball glass, the fruity peach
schnapps and orange juice concoction soothing her frazzled
nerves. "It wasn't like that with us. We. . . ." she broke off at
the skeptical arch of her friend's eyebrow.

"Honey, I'm sure that's what Gabrielle thought, too, when
they went out. And all the other girls."

Dylan wanted more than a fling. Jaine knew it deep in her
heart, but Krystal would never believe her. She viewed Dylan
the same way everyone else did. If the event debacle hadn't
happened, then perhaps over time they would have surprised
his family and friends with their connection. Instead, he
needed to prove his professional worth, and so did she.

Jaine nursed her drink, reluctant to lower it to the plastic-
flowered tablecloth until she was good and buzzed. "What a
disaster. I really wish Gabrielle hadn't raised a fuss in front
of Therese. You should have seen the way she carried on
about Dylan and me flirting and how it distracted us from our
work."

Gabrielle. She'd had a chance at the general manager job
before Dylan showed up, and she resented him for dumping
her in college. And Gabrielle had always disliked Jaine for
having the audacity to compete with her. Jaine tightened her
fingers around her glass.

"What's the matter?" At Jaine's hesitation, Krystal pressed,
"Come on, what is it?"

Unable to still her hands, Jaine twisted the side of her shirt.
"I've been so busy cleaning up this mess that it's the first time
I've had a chance to digest it. Dylan and I would never have
been this absent-minded. We both want this event to succeed

too badly. We wouldn't overlook the wrong date." Speaking the words aloud increased Jaine's conviction.

"If you guys didn't screw up, then who did?" Krystal reached down to ruffle Willow's black fur. The cat rubbed against her leg.

"Someone who wants Dylan's job, dislikes him, and has a history of being my frenemy. Think about it." During the lengthy pause, Jaine clinked ice around the bottom of the glass.

"Holy crap," Krystal burst out. "Gabrielle!"

"She also 'just happened' to walk by when we were with Therese and spill what she knew about Dylan and me. It sounded like she'd been snooping. She could have tampered with my computer files and re-sent the revised press release to the papers." Jaine sprang up and paced the kitchen. "For the flyers, she probably replaced the old stack with a new stack before they were distributed around the park."

"I'll bet you're right. If she sabotages Dylan enough, he'll lose his job and then she can step in and take his place."

"The question is how did she do it? And how do we prove it?"

Krystal chugged the rest of her drink and slapped the glass on the table. "I know how to find out."

Chapter Sixteen

Saturday night after the fireworks, Jaine accepted an offer from Sean to play miniature golf. She couldn't deal with the Gabrielle catastrophe until after the weekend so she would handle the Sean problem in the meantime. Krystal wanted to interrogate Cas, the IT Manager, about how one co-worker could hack into another's files. Unfortunately he had gone camping, and they hadn't had luck reaching him on his cell. According to Tiara, he would return to the office Monday.

For now, Jaine struggled to concentrate on playing miniature golf at the course adjacent to the Storybook Valley Inn and Grill. Tiara's parents owned it, and theme park employees received a discount.

The preschool boy ahead of them likely earned a better score than she did. Jaine couldn't stop worrying. Should she give Sean the "let's be friends talk" here? On the drive to her building?

After the game, they deposited their clubs at the exit and Sean nodded toward the snack bar. "How about an ice cream?"

"Sure. I'd love a chocolate cone. With chocolate sprinkles."

She could use an extra dose of calories to survive this dreadful weekend.

While Sean waited in line, Jaine chose a wooden bench overlooking the golf course and pressed a crease in her cargo pants. She had spent a half hour selecting an outfit that did nothing to enhance her curves.

Jaine examined a text from Bree, who had forgiven her fiancé for the open bar incident. They had compromised and limited it to the cocktail hour. Bree had sent her photos of two negligees she was considering for her wedding night: a white satin sheath and a lacy red number. Was nothing private in this world? Jaine voted for the white one, due to the bridal theme, and buried her phone back in her handbag.

Although her sister was drowning in last minute details, Bree didn't comprehend how lucky she was to have settled the most important detail of her life—choosing a partner. A golfer kissed his girlfriend alongside a retired bumper car, and Jaine bit her lip He had no inkling they'd attracted the envy of a lovesick Cinderella.

Even though Jaine had never visited the golf course, it seemed familiar after all Dylan's stories. Aunt Gretel had convinced his grandparents to donate park relics to the attraction. Along with the bumper car, Jaine had spotted putting greens showcasing an antique car, paddleboat, and Ferris wheel seat. According to Dylan, his aunt finagled a coin-operated train engine for the inn's lobby. In return, Charles made her promise to adopt four gnomes and switch the locations every two weeks. Whenever she evaded her responsibilities, Gretel found gnomes in her shower and on her pillow. Jaine had laughed when Dylan recounted the family tale during one of their phone conversations.

A wave of intense longing engulfed her. If only she was on this date with Dylan. Jaine drummed a beat against the pavement with her sandal. Why couldn't she have fallen for Sean instead of her boss? He was thoughtful. Interesting. Attractive. But they had no chemistry, and she would rather be with no guy than the wrong guy. As lonely as that sounded.

Jaine was observing a dad on his hands and knees, digging his daughter's pink ball out from a shallow creek with his golf club, when Sean offered her an ice cream cone.

He joined her on the bench, swallowed a whipped cream-doused spoonful of his sundae, and cleared his throat. "I wanted to ask you something."

Jaine busied herself with licking a sprinkle-infested path. *Please don't ask me on another date.*

"We're just friends, right?"

Jaine's mouth dropped open, and she snapped it shut before he spotted the melted chocolate. "Yes. I mean, I wasn't sure how you felt, but. . . ."

"But you're not into me."

"Um. . . ."

Sean laughed and pressed his spoon back into his sundae. "I figured that. You haven't been available for a second date in weeks. I wouldn't have asked again, but you looked upset tonight. Like you could use a friend."

Jaine released her pent-up breath, and a smile flickered to her lips. "So you thought you'd cheer me up with golf and ice cream. Thank you."

"I also wanted to tell you about my new job performing on a cruise ship. I'm leaving after Labor Day. It's not Broadway or Hollywood, but it'll help me to catch up on college loans and save money."

"That's wonderful! I'll miss you, Sean."

"Me too." Sean elbowed her. "I suspected you weren't that

into our first date when you transformed into Sleeping Beauty, but I liked hanging out with you so figured I'd try again."

"I still can't believe I dozed off. It had nothing to do with you, though, really. I was exhausted after my first week."

"Bet you wouldn't zonk out on a date with Dylan." Sean winked at her, and Jaine stared. "Come on, I'm an actor. I'm a master of non-verbal communication. I've seen how you two interact."

"Have you, uh, heard any rumors about us?"

"No. Why, did I miss anything juicy?"

Jaine swathed a napkin around her dripping cone. She could confide the whole mess, get his take on it, but Jaine decided against it. Tonight she needed a break from broken romance, betrayal, and sabotage. "No, just wondering. So tell me more about this job!"

As Sean recounted the audition details, Jaine considered inviting him to the wedding. Sean was such a nice guy that he would probably accept, but he must have hundreds of tasks to finish before starting his new job. With the Back-to-School Ball scheduled for the same evening as Bree's nuptials, he would miss part of the wedding, anyway.

Besides, Sean deserved a girl who didn't dream of dancing with someone else. Later that night, Jaine texted Bree. *Take off my plus one. Will be there alone.* She should have talked her sister into extending the open bar.

* * *

The rest of the weekend passed in a haze of bridal preparations. A notebook inside Jaine's purse reminded her of every task except when to pee. She needed to clear space in her closet so the bridesmaid gown wouldn't wrinkle, buy a white oval platter, and finish her other gift—a shadow box frame with ribbons and craft stickers arranged around the couple's cream invitation and engagement photograph.

She planned to concentrate on the Back-to-School Ball to-do list Monday afternoon after meeting with Cas. That involved reviewing the menu with Tiara, touching base with Rory over choreography and music, designing and printing personalized diplomas for each child, and gathering autograph books and souvenir pens from the park's gift shop.

Thank God her tasks distracted her from Dylan. A little bit.

Before heading into the office Monday, Jaine fetched bridesmaid gifts from the jeweler and followed her sister's orders to scrutinize each one. She hunched over the glass counter, inspecting the initial on the last bracelet. J. For Jaine.

Bree's attendants would gush over the Swarovski crystals, silver beads, dangling heart charm, and personalized initials on the bracelets, and the velvet box contained a poem thanking the bridesmaids for their support. The sentiment might have touched Jaine more if she hadn't picked up the damn things herself.

If only she could stow away on the airplane transporting Bree and Campbell to Hawaii. She would stake out a beach chair, sip from a fruity cocktail sporting a festive umbrella, and devour books on her e-reader.

Jaine sighed, capping the bracelet boxes with shiny blue lids. Instead of a trip to paradise, she needed to retrieve her own thank you gift and attend to the endless stream of messages on her phone. Jaine deemed the bracelets typo-free to the gentleman behind the counter.

He stacked the seven boxes into an embossed ivory shopping bag with handles. Her cell shrilled, and Jaine checked the number. Erin, the reporter she kept missing. She'd better take it.

"Hi, it's Jaine Andersen. Sorry for the phone tag," Jaine said, nodding her thanks to the jeweler. She strolled over to the window.

"No problem. I want to cover the ball, but I'm confused about the date. I got your revised press release, but then on your voice mail, you gave the original date."

"Revised press release?" Jaine's knees weakening, she steadied herself against a rack of pendants and necklaces. "Can you tell me who submitted it? We had a glitch at our office."

Erin placed her on hold. After a couple moments, she responded, "You sent it from your email account with a note. 'Sorry for the mix-up. The correct date should be August 29.' So is it the twenty-ninth or twenty-second?"

"Twenty-second. If you can forward that email that would be great. We're having a problem with interns. Can't trust them with anything." On impulse, Jaine added, "Is there any way you can do an advance article on the ball? This event has been jinxed. Any help getting the word out would be much appreciated."

"How about a photo? I can't promise, but I can ask whether one of our photographers is available to swing by and check out your preparations."

"Thanks, you're the best. I apologize for the confusion." Jaine hung up, and stamped her foot hard, rattling the packages in the bag.

That proved it. Someone sabotaged Cinderella's ball. And

Jaine knew the culprit. Gabrielle wasn't a stepsister, but she was uglier than anyone had anticipated.

* * *

Jaine drove as fast as possible without attracting a police escort. She logged into her email and read the forwarded message from the newspaper. Despite Erin's warning, cold shock assaulted Jaine's core. It had originated from her email address.

Only I didn't send it.

Jaine scrolled through the short list of emails in her Sent directory. Another chill shivered through her. No sign of the fraudulent message, nor her original emails to the media. She hunted through her trash folder and ran multiple searches, but found nothing.

Gabrielle went to one hell of a lot of trouble to erase evidence of her own deceit and Jaine's innocence. Had she deleted emails from Dylan's computer? When Jaine attached the original files for Dylan's approval, both included the correct date. Jaine shoved back her chair with extra force. Time to get answers.

"Something wrong, Jaine?" Therese asked from her desk. She oozed disapproval, from her curt tone to her flattened lips.

Jaine poked her tongue into her cheek and inhaled a deep breath. "I'm fine. Thanks."

As Jaine strode through the maze of cubicles, she passed Gabrielle issuing orders to the support staff. Jaine curled her fingers at her sides, tempted to jerk Gabrielle's silky ponytail, gathered in a polished gold cone holder.

Stay calm. Don't tip her off.

She retreated to Cas's cubicle in the back of the room. Jaine had seen Dylan's cousin around, but had never met the information systems manager. Wavy ginger hair covered his head and freckles dotted his cheeks. His grin and blue eyes reflected an impishness Jaine found endearing, even in her explosive state.

"Hey, Cindy, Krystal mentioned you'd be coming by to pick my brain." Cas raised a gruesome-brown wind-up brain, one of several toys peppering an otherwise neat and organized desk. "Here."

Jaine assessed the mini-basketball hoop gumball machine, wind-up toy collection, and solar dancing daisy in the window. Another quirky relative. "Um, thanks, but that's not what I had in mind."

"Hey, do you see what you did? Brain? Mind? No smile, huh? You look tense. Give this a squeeze." Cas lobbed her a squishy red robot.

Jaine compressed it and the robot sprang back between her fingers. She crushed it again. And again. Maybe she ought to get one of these things.

"I need to discuss a problem with Dylan, but first I wanted to better understand how this happened. Someone tampered with my Word files and emails."

"You're telling me we've got an actual villain in the park?" For once, Cas's grin abandoned his face.

"I know it's hard to believe, but I swear, it's the truth. I'm just wondering how many people have access to our passwords? Do supervisors?" Jaine decided against mentioning Gabrielle's name in case his friends included a corporate bitch. She wouldn't risk anyone tipping off Gabrielle.

"Nope. Just me." Cas rummaged in a desk drawer and scooped out four jointed cubes of Tetris blocks carved from the same material as the robot. He squeezed the blocks. "There are two explanations. You didn't log out before leaving your desk and someone used your computer. Or, someone used *my* computer when I stepped away and connected remotely to yours while you were logged in."

"Can we prove it?"

"The computers have logs. But they won't name our villain. We'd need an eyewitness for that. Cripes, intrigue in Storybook Valley."

"If you can check those logs that would be a start. I'll talk to Dylan. Thanks, Cas." Jaine plopped the robot back onto the desk.

"Good luck, Cindy. You're gonna need it."

Chapter Seventeen

Jaine couldn't find Dylan in the building. Hoping she would run into him, she visited Tiara in Food Services to discuss the final menu details and stopped by the gift shop for the coloring books and pens.

When Jaine returned to the office, she crouched on the floor and placed the box of books in a corner, out of the way. Therese strode over, twin red spots blooming on her cheeks. "I got your *complaint*."

Cas must have reported proof of her files getting violated. Darn, he'd promised to share evidence with Jaine first so she could break the news to Dylan.

Jaine gave the box of coloring books one final nudge against the wall before jerking upright. "I can explain. I wanted to speak to Dylan about that."

Dylan appeared in his doorway, a rigid set to his shoulders. Coldness hardened his green eyes. "I'll bet."

Her automatic surge of joy at seeing him vanished. Uneasiness quaking through her, Jaine glanced from Dylan to his mother. Her heart rate intensified at their harsh expressions. Why were they so mad? It wasn't her fault they employed a Benedict Arnold who chose her files to hack.

"We need to talk. Now." Without waiting for a reply, Dylan stalked back into his office. His mother marched in after him.

After a hesitation, Jaine shuffled forward. She joined them in time to find Dylan and his mother arguing near his desk.

"Mom, let me handle this."

"Dylan, you've gotten yourself into enough trouble," his mother snapped. "It's not wise to be alone together."

Dylan's gaze landed on Jaine and he gave a slow, disbelieving shake of his head. Raw pain etched his face. "I can't believe you did this. I thought you were different, Jaine."

He's not just angry. He's hurt.

A knot lodged in her stomach. "Please tell me what's going on."

"I shared my concerns before we started anything. You promised it wouldn't affect our professional relationship. That you'd talk to me if you were uncomfortable. I trusted you, Jaine. Then you file a sexual harassment claim behind my back." Dylan lifted a paper from his desk, his stare drilling into her.

Jaine's lungs constricted, making it difficult to breathe. "What? Let . . . let me see."

Closing the distance between them, she snatched it out of his hands. Jaine scanned the typed memo. *Unwanted advances. . .forced himself on me by the pond. . .felt my job was in jeopardy if I told someone. . .the stress from working with him has led to a decline in my job performance. . . .*

In a weak imitation of her signature, it closed with: Jaine Andersen. Ice spread through her body. Her thoughts spinning, Jaine grasped the back of a chair to keep from falling. Gabrielle. *Dylan believes I betrayed him. How could he think that?*

His distrust stung even worse than Gabrielle's lies. Blood flow rushed to her face, outrage swelling inside her.

"Jaine, although I admit this memo was disturbing, please

be assured my relationship to Dylan won't have any bearing on this investigation." Therese traced a line of sweat on her forehead. "We take harassment complaints seriously. You don't need to fear retaliation. Our procedures call for interviewing both of you separately so—"

"Dylan!" Jaine's sharp voice cut across the room. "You believe I'd betray you this way? After all the time we spent together? Do you think I'm another Tammy?"

"Tawny," Dylan muttered.

"Whatever! I'm not her." Despite her stern tone, tears filmed Jaine's vision. She squeezed them back, lashes moistening. "What possible motive would I have to hurt you?"

"You were upset when I broke up with you," Dylan countered.

"Of course I was upset. Weren't you?"

His jaw muscles flinched. "Yes. That's why I never expected you to—"

"I didn't! That's not my signature. Go talk to your cousin Cas. You'll find out someone hacked into my computer files and sabotaged the Back-to-School Ball." Jaine had a hard time speaking around the mound bobbing in her throat. "I'm not the ex-girlfriend that's out to get you, Dylan. Focus on the ex whose sights are set on the general manager job and wants nothing more than to discredit you."

Not waiting for his response, she pivoted toward a stunned Therese. Dylan's mother rocked on her feet, her bewildered gaze bouncing between her son and Jaine.

"Tomorrow I'll file a formal complaint against Gabrielle," Jaine told her, blinking hard against the smarting in her eyes. "Right now. . .I need time to prepare."

Jaine reeled out of Dylan's office, bumping into the wall

in her haste. She clocked out and stumbled toward the exit, her eyelids hot, and tears threatening to gush forth.

"Hon, are you okay?" a concerned voice asked from behind her. "You're splotchy."

Jaine swung around, the corners of her mouth pinching together. Gabrielle's ivory blouse, pleated knee-length coral skirt, and matching coral pumps suggested softness. So did her touch of blush, sheer lip gloss, and hint of eye shadow. A regular girl-next door. But Jaine knew better.

"No, Gabrielle, I am not okay, but I will be soon. You won't get away with this."

"I'm afraid I don't understand what you mean." Gabrielle flicked a hand in front of her nose as if ridding the air of a sour stench. She pressed her clipboard of support staff tasks against her chest.

"Sabotaging my press releases and flyers? A false harassment claim? Sound familiar?"

"If you can't handle your marketing job, don't blame me. Maybe you should stick to playing dress-up." Gabrielle smiled sweetly and advanced toward her desk.

Jaine's hands vibrated. She breathed in for a count of four, held it, and released a long exhale. Gabrielle wanted her to make a scene, to drive her reputation further into the ground. Jaine wouldn't allow her that satisfaction. Instead, she imagined Gabrielle under the rollercoaster, scrubbing vomit, her designer wardrobe disintegrated into rags.

* * *

When Jaine arrived home, she permitted herself ten minutes of huddling on the floor with a tissue box, her oblivious cat purring beside her. Next, she phoned Cas and verified that someone had used the IT computer to manipulate her files. She filled in Krystal on the latest developments and convinced her friend not to slash Gabrielle's tires and scrawl Psycho Bitch in red lipstick on her windshield. Although it was tempting. . . .

Jaine paced her bedroom, the air conditioner whirring in the background. "What I need you to do is find a witness who saw Psycho Bitch working on Cas's computer. He can give you the exact date and time. Can you ask around the front office?"

"Damn straight! I'll also tell Therese she's got the wrong idea, and call Dylan a jackass for not believing in you."

A pain stabbed Jaine's heart at the mention of Dylan.

"You can skip the last part, but I'd appreciate your defending me. Thanks, Krystal."

Afterwards, Jaine pored over the company's anti-harassment policy in the handbook and typed a complaint documenting Gabrielle's actions. If necessary, Jaine would seek Bree's legal advice, but first she'd present her case to Therese.

Chapter Eighteen

Jaine twisted her clammy fingers in her lap, waiting for Therese to finish studying the complaint. She readjusted her legs beneath the long glossy conference table. She hadn't known this private room existed, accessible by a Staff Only staircase in the theater building. Jaine had spent her entire Cinderella shift dreading the visit.

Therese lowered the papers onto the table and fused her gaze to Jaine. "These are strong accusations. Cas confirmed the remote use of the IT computer to access your files, so we'll investigate that along with your complaint about Gabrielle. In the meantime, please report to me rather than Dylan."

At the mention of his name, the tightness in Jaine's stomach blossomed into a series of cartwheels. She wanted to punch him in his dragon-tattooed shoulder for not trusting her, but he didn't deserve Gabrielle's spoiling his reputation. "I want to reiterate that Dylan did nothing inappropriate."

Massaging her temples, Therese sat back in her swivel chair. "I know my son wouldn't sexually harass anyone, but the general manager dating a staff member *was* inappropriate, Jaine."

"The handbook doesn't include dating policies."

"Perhaps we need to set up one regarding managers and

employees. I'm sure it was exciting to sneak around with your boss, but—"

Rising anger swelled in Jaine's chest. "I care about my career too much to jeopardize it for a casual fling. I loved. . .liked Dylan's sense of humor, and how he chats with everyone from maintenance workers to ride operators. I admire his work ethic and the way he watches out for friends and family. It warms my heart that he keeps pictures of his niece on his cell phone, playing with the pink rocking horse he bought her, and that he took *my* niece on her first rollercoaster."

Jaine also loved stroking the sexy stubble that roughened his chin and the warmth of his strong biceps around her waist. Better not mention those tidbits to his mother. "Anyway, none of that matters. We had good intentions, but it was a mistake. We're both new here and need to focus on our careers."

Besides, Dylan hadn't felt the same connection; otherwise he would have trusted her. Instead, he'd assumed the worst. The memory elicited an instant, crushing spasm of hurt. Jaine should never have confessed her feelings to Therese. She must have sounded like a lovelorn teen.

Everyone thought they knew her. Dylan equated her to Tawny. His mother considered Jaine flaky and hormonal. Her sisters saw an errand girl with no personal life. Her father only heard her good news; Jaine never confided her loneliness or struggles. Gabrielle considered her a spineless, easy target. And everyone else viewed her as Cinderella. She had transformed from plain Jaine into glamorous Cindy, but neither identity felt comfortable.

I don't even know who I am anymore.

Therese opened her mouth and then shut it. She rubbed a hand over the front of her teal blouse, tugging on a shiny pearl button. Finally, she rose and gathered the papers. "Well, then. Thank you for sharing your side. We will investigate and get back to you."

Left alone in the conference room, Jaine clasped her hands around her stiff neck.

* * *

The following morning, Jaine adjusted her Gibson Girl wig, slicked on lipstick, and regarded herself in the mirror. Done. Thank God for makeup and artificial piles of hair. They masked the circles under her eyes and lank locks she hadn't bothered washing. Bridesmaid jitters and work stress had propelled Jaine into depression.

Ugh. After all the Chunky Monkey she consumed this week, she wouldn't even fit into the Hubba Bubba gown. Jaine hauled herself up from the chair and sighed.

Krystal ambled across the dressing room, black spirals tucked beneath her red hood and her checkered skirt flaring. Her companion, Tiara, sparkled in a rhinestone headband, blue beaded blouse, and white sequined leggings.

Tiara wrenched Jaine into a side hug. "I am so sorry." She stepped back. "My brother and Krystal told me what's happening. As a family member, I feel responsible that you've been a harassment victim under our watch. I never trusted Gabrielle, and that's exactly what I told Aunt Therese."

"Me too," Krystal interjected. "I didn't want Therese's friendship with Gabrielle's mom influencing her."

"It sucks that she did this to you. I love your marketing ideas, and the ball will be fantastic." Tiara shook her head, Swarovski earrings swinging. She fumbled into a dazzling pink glitter handbag and withdrew a sheet of gold stars. "I'm sure it doesn't help, but take these, okay? Use them at the employee appreciation party. You deserve the best prize on the table."

A warm glow spread through Jaine's chest. Yes, the situation sucked, but their support touched her. "Thank you, guys. I'm lucky to have you for friends."

"We've got your back, Cindy," Krystal said. "Hang in there."

"How lovely, we all shared the same concern," a voice lilted from behind them.

Lois Callahan glided forward, bearing a pastel floral gift bag with pink satin handles. Rose tissue paper billowed over the edges. She extended the bag to a startled Jaine. "Just a thought from your fairy godmother."

Jaine reached inside and discovered the most exquisite flip flops she had ever seen. Delicate silver stones and twinkling clear jewels embellished the metallic straps. She traced her finger along the sumptuous suede lining, tissue paper crinkling. "Lois, thank you! These are beautiful."

"Everyone insists I don't know about Cinderella wearing flip flops on breaks. They forget that *I* played the role of Cinderella. Back in the day, I had to launder my own gown, and there was no backup Cinderella. I was in character seven days a week, from opening till closing. It was exhausting. I used to soak my sore feet in a tub of warm water and make Charles rub them."

Wow. Jaine had never heard Lois complain. Criticize, yes, but complain? Krystal and Tiara stared at the refined older woman before them, equally entranced.

"Anyway, at least these shoes are suitable for a princess,

not like those awful rubber ones you girls wear nowadays."
Lois fiddled with the collar of her lavender blazer.

"Aw, Gram, you've got a soft spot." Tiara gestured toward
her grandmother's flats. "And you forced Granddad to mas-
sage your feet. That's so cool."

"I can't wait to wear them." Jaine debated whether to hug
the Callahan matriarch. Maybe not. By her stiff stance, Lois
didn't expect an embrace. Instead, Jaine gathered the folds
of her gown, tucked her right foot behind her left, and bent
her knees into a curtsy.

Slowly and gracefully, Jaine resumed the upright position,
lowered her hands to her sides, and raised her head, the way
Lois had once demonstrated.

Lois nodded, approving. "Very nice, my dear. Just keep
your back a touch straighter."

She didn't mention the Gabrielle controversy, but Jaine
knew the reason for the gift. If Jaine had impressed Lois, the
park perfectionist, then perhaps she belonged in Storybook
Valley after all.

She slipped her gold stars into the bag. "I'd better get to
work. Thank you again, all of you, for your support."

On the way to the castle, Jaine exchanged waves with ride
operators, food workers, retail clerks, and even Dazzle the
Dragon. She had never met most of the people greeting her.
To the employees, she was Cinderella. They accepted her because she was one of them. *I'm okay with that.*

No, Jaine didn't want to spend her career portraying Cinderella, but she would enjoy the experience while she had it.
Krystal cherished her Red Riding Hood role, to the point that
she dressed up voluntarily, just as Lois fancied her fairy godmother character, and Tiara adored finding creative ways to

sparkle. They felt safe showing their inner quirkiness and being themselves at Storybook Valley.

Cinderella reflected sides of herself that Jaine never explored before, a playful side that coaxed her out of her comfort zone, a glamorous side that boosted her self-assurance, and a regal side that commanded respect. Fellow employees and the park's guests didn't laugh at her costume; they admired how she made children happy and presented Storybook Valley in a positive light. Jaine excelled at public relations whether planning an event or posing with children in a princess gown.

No one, not the conniving Gabrielle, suspicious Therese, or Dylan with his devastating lack of faith, would splinter her confidence.

Jaine entered the castle with new buoyancy in her step. She stopped short at the sight of a familiar white-haired elf perched atop her throne. He stood beside a blue plastic Storybook Valley bag from one of the gift shops.

Lips twitching, Jaine rustled into the bag and discovered a folded newspaper along with a gold box stamped Little Red Hen Bakery. Dylan's grandfather had scrawled "Good Job, from Filfinkle Finebang" above a newspaper photograph from the Lifestyle section. It depicted Krystal swinging at the playground with a little girl pushing her. The caption read, "Red Riding Hood will be one of many characters attending the upcoming Back-to-School Ball, where children can earn a diploma from Fairy Tale School." The second line detailed how to order tickets for the August twenty-second event.

Yes! Erin succeeded with scheduling a photographer. Jaine peeked inside the box at a soft chocolate-studded cookie, the tantalizing aroma floating up to her nostrils. She craved the cookie, but Charles Callahan's support tasted even better.

Jaine spent a busy morning greeting families, signing autographs, and leading a story time session. Holding up an illustration, Jaine noticed a woman ogling her from behind the cluster of children. Her tailored grey blazer, silk blouse, and dress pants deviated from the usual park attire. Long blonde hair cascaded in graceful waves to her shoulders. Jaine couldn't distinguish her facial features without glasses, but she resembled a fuzzy Bree. What in the name of the Brothers Grimm would Bree be doing at Cinderella story time?

The woman touched her throat, and a diamond glinted on her finger. Oh crap. Jaine didn't need glasses to see that rock. It *was* Bree.

Jaine breathed in and out three times, a relaxation technique she had learned in one of the medical center's yoga classes, but it didn't relieve the panic spiraling in her chest. Why was her sister here? Shouldn't she be preparing legal documents in her office?

Despite her thundering heart, Jaine finished the book, posed for a flurry of pictures, and thanked a girl for a crayon drawing of Cinderella's Castle. Once the last family departed, her fingers dug into the throne's armrests.

Bree strode over to her, a hand splayed across her breast. "Jaine?" she asked with a note of disbelief. "I don't believe it. *This* is your big job? Entertaining a bunch of snot-nosed kids?"

"Bree. What are you doing here?" Jaine forced the words past her stiff lips.

"What am I doing here? What about you? Are you serious? You're *Cinderella*?" Her incredulous pronunciation of Cinderella made it sound as if she'd found Jaine pimping herself out on a street corner.

"It's just temporary. I'm filling in to help them out and make extra money. My marketing position will be full-time in the fall."

"Oh, Jaine. Do you honestly think anyone will respect you after parading around in that princess get-up? You should have stood your ground. Instead, you got talked into accepting some embarrassing job meant for a high school girl."

Jaine's jaw ached from clenching her teeth. She rose, nails biting into her palms. "You know what? I'm proud of the job I'm doing here. I've fallen in love with this park and the people here, and I'm comfortable helping them out in any way I can. If it means planning an event and working with the media to attract more visitors, great."

She bent to retrieve the little girl's drawing and brandished it before her sister. Pink heart stickers bordered the castle and the crayon scribble read *I love you, Cinderella*. "But if it also means getting to dress up and seeing hundreds of little kids light up like I'm magic, I'm pretty good with that, too. I just want to be here in whatever form they need me."

Bree gave a bark of laughter. "You'd better watch out, or next they'll need you to sweep the chimney."

"Why are you even here, Bree?"

"I brought the wedding favors for you to assemble. Why didn't you tell the company to handle that? Everything came separately." Her nose wrinkled, Bree gestured to a cardboard box against the wall.

Jaine craned her neck and squinted at the packages of white Jordan almonds, silk embroidered handkerchiefs, and gold ribbons. "You didn't want to pay the extra fee, remember?" She shrugged and adjusted her silver tiara. "Wish I could help you out, but I can't. Find another slave to do your chores."

"What? Are you kidding me?" Bree sputtered, a faint tracing of red outlining her tanned cheeks. "I'm getting married this weekend. I have a million things to do."

"You shouldn't have waited until the last minute. I'm the one who arranged that delivery and I know it arrived two weeks ago. Now you have a million and one things to do." Jaine anchored a casual hand on her hip.

Bree's mouth popped open. "Fine. I don't need your help. Have fun playing *Cinderella*." She snapped up the box and bolted toward the exit.

"I will," Jaine called after her.

She returned to her throne, a sense of euphoria spreading through her.

Chapter Nineteen

Jaine finished the last bite of a bacon-wrapped sea scallop coated in tangy mustard sauce and unleashed a long sigh. Glowing, Bree squeezed her fiancé Campbell's hand and greeted guests on the brick patio. Jaine wanted happiness for her sister—even if they weren't speaking at the moment—but she couldn't deny the envy welling up inside her.

Her future brother-in-law's parents had arranged an elegant rehearsal dinner at the Mountain Ridge Lodge. Waiters circulated with platters of scallops, mini quiche, and smoked chicken quesadilla while guests enjoyed views of the lake and mountainside.

After cocktails, the group would retreat inside a rustic barn with beams latticing the ceiling and glossy wood floorboards. Jaine had seen the cake displayed on a table in the dining room, two adjoining frilly white hearts with wedding bells in the center and the couple's names inscribed in pastel blue icing. Shauna had told her that the favors complemented the cake, frosted heart cookies bearing the message *Bree plus Campbell.*

By the adoring smile Campbell cast at his almost-bride, Bree had found her happily ever after. Jaine had always envisioned her sister with the good-looking corporate type that schmoozed on golf courses, over expensive dinners, and earned six figures. Instead she'd fallen for Campbell, a pleasant-faced though not traditionally handsome, veterinarian with an Irish setter and a cat. She never wore heels anymore since they made her tower over her fiancé.

Shauna wasn't dating anyone, but she had brought a guy from her building. Jaine had spent the last ten minutes half-listening while her sisters chatted with old friends and her father and stepmother made small talk with Campbell's parents.

A warm breeze rolled through the air, rippling across the calm water. Jaine fingered the dress she had never showed off at the bachelorette party. Dylan had liked this dress.

Amber rushed over and wiggled her fingers, painted pearly pink. "Hi, Aunt Jaine. See my nails? Mom took me to a salon."

"I love it. Fancy. I'm getting mine done tomorrow." Jaine rubbed one of her bare nails.

She had made an appointment for a French manicure early the next morning. Then she would check on the Back-to-School Ball preparations, work at the castle until Wendy relieved her, change into her bridesmaid gown in Wardrobe, and meet her sisters before the ceremony.

"Why didn't you tell me you were Cinderella, Aunt Jaine? That's so cool!"

"You heard about that, huh?"

Shauna joined them as if she had bionic ears. "Of course she did. Finding out you're related to royalty is big news." She sipped from her Cosmopolitan. "So Jaine, what else have you been hiding? Should we expect a visit from your pals Snow White and Rapunzel?"

"Mom, you're so lame." Amber sent her aunt an exasperated "Can you believe her?" look.

Jaine circled an arm around her niece. Amber had earned herself a trip to the movies with a large popcorn and her favorite blue raspberry slushy.

"You never know. I mean, the annoying frumpy sisters are here." She high-fived a snickering Amber, who swiveled her head to watch her mother's reaction.

"I am *not* frumpy, Jaine." Shauna tugged at her V-neck flared red halter dress. "Or annoying. Besides, those were *step*sisters."

Jaine spotted her father waiting at the patio bar, for once detached from Gloria's hip. "I'll catch up with you later, Amber. I'm going to see Grandpa."

"Are you sure you're not running to your pumpkin coach?" Shauna retorted.

"Mooom!" Amber complained. "That's dumb."

I love that kid. Jaine strolled over to her father and greeted him with a kiss on the cheek. "How's it going, Daddy?"

He pushed back his metal-rimmed glasses, lips curved upward. He'd worn glasses Jaine's whole life; the bluish green eyes Jaine inherited came with lousy vision as a package deal. More gray speckled his brown hair than when he moved to Florida, and his daily walks around the condo complex led to a trimmer build, but his gentle smile hadn't changed.

"I'm fine. Gloria wanted a glass of wine. How about you? This is some shindig, isn't it?"

"I'm okay. Just dodging Cinderella jokes."

Bree had blabbed to the whole family, but it didn't bother Jaine the way she expected. Shauna's barbs sounded immature to an eight-year-old, and her father supported Jaine as he always had.

When her stepmother insisted she should hire a head-hunter to find a better job and blathered about her successful children who earned six figure incomes, Jaine mentally reviewed her to-do list for tomorrow.

Perhaps she owed Gabrielle a thank you. After being framed for incompetence and a sexual harassment allegation, and witnessing how little your boyfriend trusted you, all other insults seemed trivial.

Her father accepted a crystal glass from the bartender and motioned for Jaine to follow. They drifted over to a row of hedges strewn with white lights. "Your mother would have loved seeing you entertain kids in a Cinderella gown. She'd be so proud of you."

"Proud? Why?"

"Because you took a risk and went after your goals. You put yourself out there, trying something new even if it's not comfortable. Besides, spending a summer in costume sounds fun. You deserve to have fun." His wistful glance spanned the festivities. "Enjoy yourself while you're young, honey. Time goes fast. Seems like yesterday that Bree wet her pants in third grade and your mother had to bring in a change of clothes."

"Thanks, Daddy." Emotion thickened Jaine's voice. Then she registered the full meaning of her father's words and her burgeoning tears subsided. "Wait a minute. Did you say *third grade?*"

"Next time Bree gives you a hard time about Cinderella, why don't you remind her. I'll bet she'd do anything to keep it quiet." Winking, her father patted her shoulder.

Jaine chuckled. "Did I ever tell you how much I love you?"

***

"There." Krystal slid the last pin into Jaine's hair and spritzed a cloud of spray onto the loose bun with a braided wrap. Behind them, the Gingerbread Man feigned coughing and Dazzle the Dragon smacked him on the back. In a far corner, the Jack and Jill actors rehearsed choreography with Rory. The ball would begin soon, but Jaine needed to leave for the wedding.

She inspected her appearance in the dressing room mirror. Bree wouldn't like the glasses in her pictures, but Jaine had resolved that it wasn't her sister's decision. Without them, she risked slighting relatives and old family friends by not recognizing anyone through the hazy blur. Her sister should approve of the elegant hairstyle, expertly applied makeup, and polished nails, though, and the gold-rimmed crystal earrings that accented Jaine's engraved bracelet.

"Thanks, Krystal. If only I wasn't in Tutti Frutti." Jaine vacated her chair, pinching a hot pink ruffle.

"Stop worrying! I love my costume, but I'd trade for a chance to wear that gown. I agree with your sisters. It's gorgeous, especially on you. Just don't forget to switch shoes." Krystal adjusted her own curls before the mirror, red cape flowing around her shoulders.

"Thanks for your help getting ready. I'm so jittery, I can't sit still." Jaine dropped her brush into the tote bag that contained her accessory boxes, dyed pumps, and dressy metallic clutch.

She scooped out her clutch and retrieved the to-do list in her wallet. Jaine paced in her Cinderella slippers, rereading the Back-to-School Ball tasks. After the newspaper photo ran, several last minute reservations arrived. Throughout the week, she'd reviewed meal counts with Tiara, watched a dress rehearsal of Rory's production, approved the set design, and delivered personalized diplomas to Lois, who would hand them out as Fairy Godmother. She counted coloring books and pens twice to make sure they had enough supplies.

"Will you relax?" Krystal asked. "You must be exhausted after running around all morning and then playing Cinderella. You've got a long night."

"Tell me about it." Jaine couldn't wait to finish the nerve-wracking walk up the aisle. She would unwind during the reception and tune out the dozens of couples slow-dancing around her. She'd mingle and enjoy the wedding cake.

Hopefully the bakers hadn't spit in the frosting. Over the past several months, Bree had changed her mind multiple times, vacillating from carrot cake, to lemon, to red velvet, to coconut with lime. Jaine convinced her sister to settle on white chocolate with raspberry, showing her a magazine article that described the combination as "classy and traditional with a surprising burst of fruity flavor."

She and her sister hadn't spoken during the rehearsal though Campbell hugged Jaine and thanked her for coordinating the wedding preparations. He apologized for Bree's behavior, calling her "a little stressed." Jaine wouldn't tarnish her sister's wedding day with tension between them, so she'd have to be the bigger person. Once again.

"Jaine." Rory crossed the room, cell phone cupped in her hand. "Dylan texted me. He asked if you could meet him in his office."

A shot of adrenaline jumped through her body. Communication from Dylan? Jaine hadn't seen or talked to him all week.

"I'll be right there." She folded the list back into her clutch. "Break a leg, guys. Um, not literally. Not at my event."

"We've got it covered. Go have fun." Krystal shooed her out the door.

Dylan waited in his office, thick gold hair falling on his forehead. Jaine's heart cinched and she couldn't steady her erratic pulse. She vowed to stay nonchalant even though electricity charged the air.

"I'm heading to the wedding unless you need something else."

His gaze zeroed in on her. "That can't be the horrible bridesmaid gown you told me about. . .Jaine, you look amazing."

"You shouldn't say things like that. I could accuse you of sexual harassment." Bitterness spilled over into her voice.

They stared at each other across a sudden ringing silence.

Dylan bowed his head and then raised it. "I'm sorry I was so quick to believe the worst. I'd been hurt before, and it felt like no matter how hard I tried, I couldn't get my life back on track. After I met you, it finally seemed like things were going right, but I kept waiting for the other shoe to drop. And then it did."

"Except I'm not the one who dropped it."

"I know. Once I got over the shock, I knew you would never write that letter. I just needed time to investigate." Dylan paused, a hard set to his jaw line. "That's why I called you in here. We fired Gabrielle."

Her breath stilled in her lungs. "What? Really?"

"A witness placed her at Cas's desk at a time that matched the logs. When we confronted her, Gabrielle insisted she did nothing wrong because I was incompetent and she deserved my job. My mother's escorting her to the parking lot right now."

Gabrielle Allaire fired. Jaine's lips twitched with a suppressed smile, her shock morphing into exhilaration. She would savor this news tonight over a slice of white chocolate with raspberry cake.

"I'm sorry you got stuck in the middle," Dylan said. "I hope we can put this behind us and continue working together."

Jaine gave a slow nod. "I'd like that. Let's just forget about it. . .forget about everything."

The last word pummeled her square in the chest. She could never erase the heady memories of his lips exploring hers or the easy way they talked and joked, but Jaine had to try. Perhaps in time, the hurt would fade.

His eyes riveted on her. "I don't know if I can forget."

An apprehensive thrill coursed through Jaine and her brows winged upward. *Stay strong.* Dylan might find her attractive, but he wasn't seeking a serious relationship, not when he had gained another chance at managing the family business. Jaine had won her reputation back, and she wouldn't endanger it again.

"I have to get to the wedding," Jaine murmured.

"Jaine—"

"Goodbye, Dylan." She left him standing in the middle of the office.

When Jaine reached the staff lot, she glimpsed Gabrielle

behind the wheel of a parked Toyota, the window open. Jaine fished her keys out of her clutch and lingered beside Psycho Bitch.

A true princess would resist a snarky comment. Good thing Jaine wasn't a true princess. "Going somewhere?"

Gabrielle glared at her over the top of her sunglasses. "I'm leaving this stupid place."

"Oh, that's right. I heard you got fired."

"Where are *you* going, Jaine? The prom? Don't you need a wrist corsage?" Gabrielle's chin notched up, she gauged Jaine's outfit.

"I'm done with high school stuff. I've matured since then. Too bad you can't say the same." Jaine leaned closer to the window. "Have fun job-hunting, Gabrielle. Here's a tip. Don't use the employers you sabotaged as references."

How ironic. Gabrielle's face colored Tutti Frutti.

Chapter Twenty

Panting, Jaine burst into the changing room. Bridesmaids milled in small clusters and her niece huddled over a hand-held video game in the corner. "Sorry I'm late. I was double-checking the decorations."

Bree and Campbell would wed outdoors at the reception site. Treetops fringed rows of ivory folding chairs and brilliant flowers bloomed along both sides. Jaine had counted chairs, inspected the garland draping the gazebo's archway and chiffon ribbons wrapped around the pillars, and made sure that rose petals flanked the aisle runner. Her father urged her inside the building, assuring her he had the situation under control.

Bree spun to face her, breathtaking in a strapless A-line gown with a beaded lace bodice and soft tulle skirt. Sequins embellished the train flowing a few feet behind her. Tiny curling tendrils escaped her classic braided chignon. Jaine had seen her sister in the wedding dress before, but today Bree glowed with ethereal radiance.

Jaine gasped. "Oh, Bree. You look—"

"Like a princess?" Bree asked.

Seriously? Cinderella cracks now? Wasn't Bree fretting over the anxieties that burdened normal brides, like tripping over her train, spilling wine on her gown, or squatting over a toilet?

Don't kill her. It's her wedding day.

"I never realized how amazing it felt being a princess," Bree continued before Jaine could craft a response. "Campbell told me I shouldn't have judged you. I'm sorry about that. And I get it now!"

She did?

Jaine goggled at the strange words emanating from her sister's mouth. "You do?"

"It's amazing having everyone pamper you and admire your beauty. To be the center of attention. Now I understand why you enjoy dressing up as Cinderella. It's like you're a bride every day!"

Jaine blinked behind her glasses. "What about the groom, gifts, and honeymoon?"

"Bree, we need to put on your veil," Shauna interrupted, ushering her twin to a chair. Her rhinestone-embellished pumps, dyed hot pink to match her dress, clicked across the tiled floor.

The shoes! Jaine's heart did the Macarena in her chest. Her gaze slid down to her glass slippers, confirming what she suspected. Crap! She'd left her tote bag in Wardrobe. Dylan's summons must have diverted her attention.

Okay, maybe no one would notice. Really, who looked at the bridal party's feet during a wedding?

Guests who needed relief from blinding Tutti Frutti evening gowns, that's who.

All right, she needed a plan. Krystal. If Jaine texted her, Krystal could deliver the bag after the Back-to-School Ball. Possibly in time for the photo shoot.

Jaine whisked her cell phone out of her clutch and tapped

a frantic message. *Help! Wrong shoes! Can u bring my bag after ball? At Candle Ridge Inn. XO*

There. Her friend wouldn't get the message until later—Red Riding Hood didn't carry a cell phone—but at least she'd tried.

"Are you ready for a perfect wedding, ladies?" Bree asked.

Shauna fussed behind her, adjusting the mid-length veil.

Jaine tugged down the sides of her dress as if she could magically conceal her ankles. "Sure am. Let me go admire that veil from the back."

***

Warm tears pooling against Jaine's lashes, she walked down the aisle, arm-in-arm with Campbell's younger brother. Her father teared up during the vows and that prompted Jaine's waterworks. She clutched her bold fuchsia bouquet of roses, tulips, calla lilies, and hydrangeas, wishing she could raise it to hide her face, or lower it to shield her shoes.

Bree and her new husband greeted friends and relatives with the landscaped gardens and mountain ridges forming an impressive backdrop. Off to the right, waitresses laid out platters of hors d'oeuvres onto a buffet table. While guests mingled in the courtyard, the bridal party would pose for the photographer before the trellis, gazebo, fountains, and rose bushes. Afterwards, everyone would retire to the grand ballroom with its glittering chandeliers and glass wall fronting the mountains.

Her usher excused himself to join his wife, leaving Jaine

alone in a sea of wedding-goers. Hot, heavy air rolled over her, reeking of Aqua Net, perfume, and flowers. She debated whether to snatch an abandoned program and fan herself. Guests had fluttered programs throughout the ceremony, desperate to cool off. Rather than Swedish meatballs and skewered Chicken Saltimbocca, this place needed a Popsicle and Italian ice station.

"Jaine."

Heat slammed through her from the inside as her eyes fastened on Dylan's long lean frame. His midnight black suit, cut to precision, fell in fine lines to his black leather shoes. He carried her dyed wedge pumps, sunlight dazzling the rhinestones in the center.

She squinted in the brightness. "Dylan. What. . .what are you doing here?" Weak from thirst, her emotional state, and shock, she lowered herself into a chair in the last row.

"You forgot something." His gaze welded onto her face then slowly skimmed down her body to her Cinderella slippers.

"My shoes. Thank you."

"That's not what I meant. You forgot to take a wedding date." Drops of moisture clung to his forehead, whether from nerves or humidity, she couldn't tell.

She turned away, her posture stiff. "Dylan, we broke up for a reason."

"A stupid reason. You're more important to me than Storybook Valley. Jaine, I don't want to lose you."

"But your parents. . . ."

"Saw how miserable I was. When my mom heard I was going after you, she chased after me with the shoes. Her exact words were, 'That girl deserves a Prince Charming. Go get her.'" Dylan crouched on the grass. His fingers cupping her ankle, he lifted off one glass slipper.

He looked up from the ground. "Jaine, you're beautiful, kind, generous, hard-working, smart, and funny. I was a jerk. Please give me another chance. I've fallen in love with you."

Her throat dry, Jaine absorbed his hopeful expression. She had always wanted a fairy tale ending, but maybe that was an illusion. Cinderella and her prince shared the most superficial relationship in history. In real relationships, partners quibbled over whether to have an open bar at their wedding. Her own parents had bickered over squeezing the toothpaste from the middle or the end and proper dishwasher loading technique.

She and Dylan experienced a rough start, but they loved each other. And that was all that mattered. Well, that and whether the shoe fit.

Jaine jiggled her toes, the nails shimmering hot pink. "Let's leave it up to fate. I believe you wanted to return something?"

A familiar grin teased the corners of his mouth. She shivered, despite the humidity.

"We've got to prove they belong to you first. No offense, but I'm not sure your feet are dainty enough."

Laughter floated up to Jaine's throat. "Hey! Aren't you supposed to be charming?"

"Sorry, sweetheart, with me you're getting a scoundrel." Dylan eased her foot into the satin open-toed pump. Pleats and a rhinestone ornament adorned the top. "What do you know? We have a match."

Applause and catcalls thundered behind them. Jaine swung around in her seat. Her father, stepmother, sisters, new brother-in-law, niece, the bridesmaids, and Great Aunt Jane clapped in unison while the videographer recorded away. Great, now the family could relive her private romantic moment forever.

"Hi Dylan! I knew you'd come!" Amber shouted, flinging the last red petals from her organza basket.

"Hey kiddo." Dylan straightened to his full height. "Don't you look pretty."

Bree sailed toward them, her train rippling. Shauna bent to flatten the embroidered folds. "I can't believe you wore Cinderella slippers during my wedding! Your glasses are bad enough."

"Dylan, meet Bree." Jaine yanked her sweaty tired foot out of the other slipper, pressed it into the dyed shoe, and popped up.

She would allow her sister one insult due to the whole being-the-bride thing, but if Bree dispensed further abuse, the third grade soaked pants incident might come out during a toast.

"Congratulations." Dylan offered Bree an adorable sheepish smile. "Sorry to crash your wedding. Don't worry about putting me somewhere. All I want is to dance with Jaine."

A rosy tint flooded Jaine's cheeks as he looped her hand in his.

Bree waved him off, her diamond ring sparkling. "No problem. I included Jaine's plus one in the count. Just in case. Miracles happen, right?"

Jaine didn't know whether to hug her sister or smother her with the veil.

"What she means is, we're glad to have you here," Campbell interjected, nudging his bride.

"Yes, welcome. You'll be at my dad's table. For now, I need to steal your Cinderella." Bree towed Jaine's arm, signaling the photographer and his assistant to follow them toward a trellis.

"Jaine, he's cute!" Shauna whispered, grasping the end of the train.

Jaine glanced back at Dylan, talking with her father. He sure was.

***

After the reception, Dylan followed Jaine to her apartment. They had managed a few slow dances and a short walk around the grounds, but every five minutes someone disturbed them. Extended family members barged in with small talk, her stepmother complained about Northeast winters and couldn't fathom Dylan's attraction to skiing, a bored Amber solicited Tic-Tac-Toe companions, Bree needed help in the bathroom.

Even Krystal and Rory intruded. First they texted Dylan about whether 'he had gotten the girl.' When he replied yes, Jaine's phone pealed with excited queries. They wouldn't quit until Jaine sent a selfie of her and Dylan dancing.

Jaine flipped on the kitchen light and smiled. The minute hand on the clock had ticked to 11:59. How fitting.

"Alone at last." His tone husky, Dylan bridged the gap between them.

His mouth moved over hers in a smoldering kiss that sent her blood pumping. Dylan slipped off her glasses, leaned over, and folded them onto the table. "As much as I like these, they're in my way. How blind are you without your glasses?"

Goosebumps prickled on her skin as she recognized one of the first questions he had ever asked her.

"I take them off for special occasions," she murmured. "When I feel like it."

His lips advanced again and Jaine sank her fingers through his hair. Dylan's lips explored her neck.

"Didn't you tell me you were tired of fooling around with Cinderella?" Jaine whispered.

"Not anymore. I'm just getting started." Dylan's hands slipped up to her bare arms, edging her closer.

As the clock struck midnight, they merged into another kiss.

THE END

Thank you for taking the time to read *Fooling Around With Cinderella*. If you enjoyed this book, please consider telling your friends and posting a short review. Word of mouth is an author's best friend and much appreciated. Thank you!

Acknowledgements

Once upon a time, a mystery writer wanted to branch into a new direction and create a light and sparkly romantic comedy series set in a fairy tale theme park. She wanted to invite readers on a mental vacation to a special place called Storybook Valley where they could bond with quirky characters and return now and then to catch up on the latest happenings. She wishes to extend her deepest appreciation to all those who have helped on her latest writing adventure. . .

To my editor Jen Malone – My fairy godmother must have been working overtime that fateful day I picked up your bookmark at that small July 4th parade. Who would have thought going to that parade would have such a significant impact not only on *Fooling Around With Cinderella*, but on the series as a whole? Thanks so much for the brainstorming and for helping me to get the creative juices flowing again. You truly understood what I was trying to accomplish and how I needed to approach it. And thanks for the gnome idea!

To Joanne Braley – My lifelong friend who has been my first beta reader since we were about twelve. Thank you for reading all those Cinderella drafts, for your fantastic catches, and for always coming through for me.

To Elaine Raco Chase – I am so grateful to have such a successful romantic comedy author, and truly amazing person, in my corner. Thank you for all the cover concept brain-storming, for your valuable beta reader feedback, and for gently reminding me that "said" is not an invisible word!

To Christina Greer – You are an inspiring teacher, the kind that your students will always remember for making a difference, as well as a talented writer and editor. Thank you for your insightful feedback, which obviously had a profound impact on the opening pages of this book. Any author is lucky to have you on their team.

To Dale Furse and Carol Baier – Thank you to two wonderful writers for your beta reading and feedback. It's much appreciated.

To all my editing clients – Thank you for trusting me with your novels, for your wonderful testimonials and word of mouth, and for helping me to keep my creativity and editing skills sharp. I am honored to have the privilege of playing in your fictional worlds and am always proud to see your books in print.

To my parents, Fran and Larry Drumtra – Thank you for all your encouragement and support over the years. I wouldn't be where I am without you. Thank you for all the proofreading, book promotion support, babysitting, for the beautiful new rug and my favorite recliner, and so much more.

To my mother-in-law and father-in-law, Claire and Steve Juba – Thank you for always asking how the writing is going, for spreading the word about new books, for diabetes camp, and for the countless other ways you help us.

To Mark Juba, my husband, graphic designer, and Prince Charming – Thank you for giving me a real life happily ever after starting with a proposal in Disney World and a honeymoon excursion to Disneyland Paris. Thanks for always be-lieving in me, for your amazing book cover designs, and for always coming through for me when I need covers resized, book promo materials designed, and editorial feedback. Looking forward to many more theme park trips!

To Lauren and Caitlin, who much prefer flip flops to glass slippers – You're both beautiful princesses, inside and out, and I am looking forward to watching you find your happily ever after. Wishing you lots of magic and fairy dust to make all your dreams come true.

About the Author

Stacy Juba got engaged at Epcot Theme Park and spent part of her honeymoon at Disneyland Paris, where she ate a burger, went on fast rides, and threw up on the train ride to the hotel. In addition to working on her Storybook Valley chick lit/sweet romance series, Stacy has written books about ice hockey, teen psychics, U.S. flag etiquette for kids, and determined women sleuths. When she's not visiting theme parks with her family, (avoiding rides that spin and exotic hamburgers), or writing about them, Stacy helps authors to strengthen their manuscripts through her Crossroads Editing Service. She also teaches online classes for writers on blogging, time management, and editing skills. Stacy is the founder of the Glass Slipper Sisters, a group of authors with Cinderella-themed romance novels. She is currently writing the next book in the Storybook Valley Series, *Prancing Around With Sleeping Beauty.*

Sink or Swim

By Stacy Juba
Available in paperback, e-book and audiobook editions

Cassidy Novak stared into the seething water. It couldn't end this way.

Gray waves buffeted against the 179-foot schooner and fog billowed through the spiderweb of rigging that snarled skyward. Heavy white sails furled, the Atlantic Devil's triple masts lumbered in formation like dead trees.

Gabriel stalked from the bow to mid-ship, his black turtleneck and slacks contrasting with his pale face. Cassidy's pulse hammered in her throat as she searched his sober expression.

His full lips curled into what would have been a grin for most people. For Gabriel, the Grim Reaper, it mimicked a sneer.

He withdrew a saber from the metal sheath belted at his waist and gripped the hilt beneath the curve of the scoop-shaped hand-guard. Above the main mast, the black and white skull and crossbones flag thrashed in a wind dance.

Cassidy glanced at Reggie, the last surviving competitor besides herself. He rubbed the back of his shaved head and connected his fingers behind his neck. Her own posture locked tight. One of them would go home a millionaire.

The other ... she wouldn't reflect on that.

After three months isolated from society on the new reality show Sink or Swim, Cassidy wanted that prize money and the fame that accompanied it. Hope fortified her very bones. Maybe her days of scrambling to pay off debts and working a lousy job were over.

It's yours. It has to be.

Just then, Gabriel caught her eye and gestured over his shoulder. Cassidy followed his index finger toward the gangway. To the plank.

Cassidy's daredevil smile, practiced in the mirror before setting sail, faded like mist.

Her clever comebacks, which she'd imagined quoted at the water coolers of America, were not heard.

Her cascading red hair that she'd tossed like a drama queen – an invention strictly for TV – went taut around her finger.

She'd lost. The overall point tallies had come in, and she'd lost. Her dreams weren't coming true after all.

"Game over. You lose. Close call though, Reggie beat you by five points." Gabriel dragged her across the deck by the arm and pushed her up onto the wooden board that projected over the water.

Cassidy winced, emptiness invading her body like a physical hurt. Five points. If only she hadn't screwed up furling and unfurling sails during the first episode, or if she'd done a better job mopping the deck that time she had a cold. After all Cassidy had been through, two simple mistakes cost her the game.

48224692R00136

Made in the USA
Charleston, SC
28 October 2015